WHERE HAVE ALL THE PARENTS GONE?

Other Avon Camelot Books in the
SPINETINGLER *Series*
by M. T. Coffin

(#1) THE SUBSTITUTE CREATURE
(#2) BILLY BAKER'S DOG WON'T STAY BURIED
(#3) MY TEACHER'S A BUG

Coming Soon

(#5) CHECK IT OUT—AND DIE!

SPINETINGLERS

#4

WHERE HAVE ALL THE PARENTS GONE?

M. T. COFFIN

AN AVON CAMELOT BOOK

WHERE HAVE ALL THE PARENTS GONE? is an original publication of Avon Books. This work has never before appeared in book form.

AVON BOOKS
A division of
The Hearst Corporation
1350 Avenue of the Americas
New York, New York 10019

First Avon Camelot Printing: July 1995

CAMELOT TRADEMARK REG. U.S. PAT. OFF. AND IN OTHER COUNTRIES, MARCA REGISTRADA, HECHO EN U.S.A.

Printed in the U.S.A.

OPM 10 9 8 7 6 5

PROLOGUE

For some reason, I knew even before I opened the front door that I was going to have this really awful argument with Mom.

"Is that you, Mary?"

"Yes, Mom, it's me." Who else was she expecting? I wondered. An alien from another planet?

"I'm in the kitchen. Please come here a minute, dear." She was using *that* tone of voice—a tone I couldn't stand.

I laid my books on the sofa and went into the kitchen. Mom was standing at the counter, drinking a cup of coffee and mixing something in a bowl. "What's wrong?"

"Sweetheart, I saw you coming down the sidewalk just now, and you have to do something about your posture. It's terrible. You're going to be stoop-shouldered by the time you get out of the sixth grade if you don't straighten up."

Good grief! Why couldn't Mom be like those old-fashioned television mothers and welcome me home from school with milk and cookies, instead of a lecture about posture? Actually, I knew why. She was bored out of her mind playing housewife here in Broxton.

"I try, Mom, but I feel like a basketball player sometimes."

"Well, you are a bit taller than the rest of the girls in your class, but you're still very pretty."

I sighed. Not this again. "Thanks for sharing that," I said.

"I made an appointment to have your hair done Friday afternoon."

"Why? I like my hair the way it is!"

"Oh, Mary, all you ever do is wear it parted in the middle, with those awful metal barrettes on each side!"

That did it! "You and Dad are always on my case about something! You're driving me crazy. Sometimes I wish you'd both just disappear. The way you two use your brains, you'd probably be better off if you didn't even have them!"

I turned and ran out of the kitchen.

"Mary!"

"I'm not hungry for dinner, either," I shouted over my shoulder, "so don't bother to call me!"

When I got upstairs to my room, I slammed the door and threw myself down on my bed.

I may go down to breakfast in the morning, I thought, and then again, I may not!

Whatever it was, it had a huge head and two huge eyes, and it was coming toward me, saying, "I want your brain! I need your brain!"

"No!" I screamed at it.

I turned and tried to run, but my feet wouldn't move.

"I want your brain!" the *thing* kept saying. "I need your brain!"

Far away, I could hear a ringing sound. Someone was at our front door. "Help me!" I cried. "Help me!"

The *thing* was getting closer now. "I want your brain! I need your brain."

Suddenly, the ground beneath my feet gave way, and I began falling into blackness.

I hit bottom with a thud.

"Ouch!"

I opened my eyes. It took me a minute to realize that I was on the floor, tangled up in my sheets. I had fallen out of bed.

3

It had all been a bad dream.

Downstairs, I could still hear the ringing, but it was the telephone, not the door bell.

I lay there for several seconds, trying to come to grips with what had just happened to me, wishing, too, that either Mom or Dad would answer the stupid telephone, because the ringing was driving me nuts.

If I had a phone in my room, I could answer it. My parents had decided that I could use the one in the kitchen or the den until I got to high school. The one in their bedroom was off-limits.

The telephone continued to ring.

"I'd answer the phone if I had one in my room!" I screamed, as I began struggling to untangle myself.

Finally, I was free of the sheets and able to stand up. I went to the door and shouted, "Mom, Dad, answer the telephone!"

Still, it continued to ring.

Now, I was more puzzled than irritated. "Mom? Dad?" I ran downstairs to the kitchen and grabbed the receiver. "Hello!"

"What took you so long, Mary?" It was my best friend Pattie Chambers.

"I thought my parents would get it. Usually, the slightest noise wakes them up."

"Are they there?"

"Is who here?"

"Your parents. Are they there?"

4

"Of course they're here, Pattie. Why wouldn't they be?"

"Mine aren't. I got up this morning, and they weren't anywhere around."

"Hold on, then. I'll go check."

I laid down the receiver and ran toward my parents' bedroom, which is on the first floor of our house. The door was open, which surprised me, so I didn't have to knock. They weren't in their bed, but I could tell it had been slept in.

"Mom? Dad?" I cried out to the rest of the house. No answer. It was weird.

I ran from room to room, frantically flinging doors open and calling my parents. I even looked in the garage. Now I was really getting scared.

Then I raced back upstairs, where I did the same thing again. My parents weren't anywhere in the house.

Downstairs again, I looked out the kitchen window to see if they were in the backyard. They weren't. They weren't in the front yard, either.

I ran back to the telephone. "No, Pattie, my parents aren't here, either, and it's all my fault!"

"What do you mean?"

"I had this really awful argument with Mom yesterday after school. I was really awful! I even said I wished she and Dad would disappear! Now they have!"

"Oh, Mary, I don't know what to do."

"I'll be right over." I hung up the receiver and ran back upstairs to get dressed. I put on my clothes, ran a comb through my hair, and brushed my teeth.

Out front, I noticed a strange stillness. There was absolutely no one around.

I started running.

Two blocks from our house, the four-year-old Thompson twins were wandering around their front yard in their pajamas. I baby-sat them almost every weekend.

"David! Daniel! What are you doing out here? Where are your parents?"

David's face was streaked with tears. "I want Mama and Daddy," he sobbed.

"What is going on around here?" I wondered aloud. I took them both by the hand. "You guys are coming with me."

Pattie lived ten blocks away and by the time I reached her house, I had three other kids with me—Jimmy Oaks, Andy James, and Cindy Montgomery.

Pattie's front door was open. "Pattie!" I called.

She came running down the stairs and stopped dead when she saw the five kids. "What's going on, Mary? Why did you bring them with you?"

"They were wandering the streets," I said in a low voice. "Their parents are gone, too."

That did it for Pattie. She lost it. Of course, when the little kids saw this, they started crying, too.

I finally got everyone calmed down. "Okay now. We've got to figure out what we need to do." I thought for a second. Nothing came to mind. Then we heard horns honking outside. I ran over to the window and looked out. "Oh, great. This is just great."

Pattie joined me. "What's wrong?"

A couple of high school kids were speeding up and down the street in their cars. "Their parents must have disappeared, too. They're probably thrilled to death." This doesn't look good at all, I thought. "Do you think all the parents in town have just disappeared?"

"How could that happen? How could they just *disappear*?"

"I haven't the faintest idea, but I can't believe that every parent in town would vanish just because I got mad at mine. There has to be more to it than that."

Pattie was wringing her hands now. "I'm scared, Mary. I'm really scared."

"I'm scared, too," I said.

Two more cars came racing down her street, honking wildly.

"They're going nuts out there, Pattie," I said. "We've got to do something about this, before things get completely out of control."

7

"Like what?"

"First, let's call all the kids in our class to see if their parents have disappeared, too. If they have, we'll get them to meet us in the town square and try to figure out what to do together."

Unlike mine, Pattie's parents let her have her own phone, so after we got the little kids interested in a TV show, we started calling.

Our town is really small, so there's only one school, and it goes from kindergarten through twelfth grade. Our class, the sixth grade, has the most kids—twenty. Some of the high school classes only have three or four students.

In just a little over an hour, we reached all twenty kids. All their parents were gone, too!

We woke up most of them. Without their parents to get them out of bed on a school day, they had overslept. For most of the others, the ones who were already awake, what had happened just hadn't sunk in yet. It never occurred to them that because their parents weren't at home, they had disappeared. That's mainly because we don't live in a normal town.

Broxton's in the middle of Nevada. The only way in or out is by airplane. Of course, I guess you could hike out, if you knew where the mine fields were located, so you wouldn't get blown up. Actually, it's isolated on purpose, because most of our parents work on top secret projects for the United States government. (The others run the schools and the stores or, like Mom, just stay home and take care of us kids.) We have the highest number of Ph.D.'s per capita of any town in the United States. No one else in the country knows this, though, because no one else in the country knows our town exists. It's really strange, if you stop to think about it, which most of us kids try not to do. When we do think about it, what we think about is *leaving*!

Pattie and I gave the little kids some cookies and then together we all headed out the door toward the town square to meet the rest of the kids in our class. The street racers weren't anywhere around.

"What do you think happened to them?" Pattie whispered.

"I hope they ran out of gas!"

"No. No. I mean our parents. What do you think happened to them?"

"I don't know, Pattie. I'm as puzzled by this as you are. That's why I wanted us all to get together. Maybe some of the other kids will have an idea."

"I hope so." She looked at me. Then she said something we'd both avoided saying: "You don't think they're all dead, do you?"

I frowned and shook my head at her, trying to get her not to talk so loud. I didn't want the little kids thinking about what might have happened to their parents, which was dumb, I guess, because pretty soon they'd all start wondering about their parents again and why they weren't at home doing the things they usually did.

The closer we got to the town square, the more kids began to appear. Kyle Paretsky, Harland Elkins, Aaron Charlaine, and Nancy Sandford crossed the street and got in step with us.

"How could they all just disappear?" Nancy said. I could tell she'd been crying, too.

I shrugged. "Did any of you hear noises during the night?"

They all shook their heads.

"I didn't, either, but I did have a really awful nightmare." I laughed. "There was this strange creature with a huge head and two huge eyes coming at me." I stopped, because now I was suddenly beginning to feel silly for even having mentioned it, so I decided to skip the part about the creature wanting my brain.

"Whoever took our parents may have invaded your thoughts," Harland said.

"You both read too much science-fiction," Kyle told him.

"At least I can read!" Harland shot back.

"Okay, you two," I said. "We've got to stick together in this. We can't go nuts like the high school guys have done."

"What do you mean?" Aaron said.

"They've been racing up and down my street like crazy all morning," Pattie told them.

"Sounds like fun to me," Aaron said.

It would, I thought, but I didn't say anything, because we had reached the town square. There were more than fifty kids there, so some others besides the ones we called must have found out about the meeting.

"Come on, Mary!" Sam Yorke shouted. "You got us down here. Tell us what we're supposed to do."

I wasn't quite sure what I was going to say, but Sam was right, so I made my way through the crowd to one of the park benches. I stood up on it, even though it made me feel like I was on stilts, and looked out at the faces of all the kids. They were all looking at me, as though I had a really great plan to get our parents back, but I didn't. In fact, I had absolutely no idea what to do, so I just opened my mouth to see what would come out. Before I could say anything, though, a couple of cars came racing together down the street. They both practically turned the corner on two wheels.

"See! If we don't work together to try to solve this, more things like that will happen."

"They'd do that anyway," someone shouted.

"I know," I said, "but now there won't be any consequences. It'll only get worse, too."

"But what can we do?" someone else shouted.

I was thinking fast now. "The first thing we need to do is get the really young kids together with

11

some of us older kids. There are three new babies in town that I know of."

"That's right, and I have two of them with me," Clara Conners called. I could see now that she was pushing a stroller back and forth.

"Good," I said. "I think we should make a list of the young kids and then divide them up among us."

Over the next few minutes, we figured out how many little kids were still at home, then I assigned at least one older kid to go get them and take them to their houses. Pattie and I kept David and Daniel, but we gave up the three other kids.

"I think we should all stay together in one house," Clara said. "What if they try to kidnap all of us tonight?"

"Yeah!" several people shouted.

"Wait a minute! Wait a minute! We don't even know for sure that's what happened to our parents," I said, "but if it did, then I think whoever did it would have kidnapped us last night, too."

"Maybe they didn't have room for everyone," Clara insisted. "Maybe they're coming back tonight!"

Everyone in the crowd was beginning to get upset, just thinking about all the things that could happen to us. A lot of the little kids started to cry.

Pattie joined me on the park bench. "Stop it! Stop it!" she shouted. "We've got to stick together!"

"Thanks," I whispered.

12

"I'm feeling better," she whispered back.

I turned back to the crowd. "Look, we don't know what happened. All right? We just know that our parents are missing. Nobody saw them leave. When we got up this morning, they were gone."

The sobs continued, but they didn't seem as loud.

"Do you all have enough to eat in your houses?" Pattie shouted.

"Yes," everyone called back.

I spotted Tim Luland at the back of the crowd. His father ran the only grocery store in town. His mother had a Ph.D. in physics. "Tim, if we need food, do you have the key to the grocery store?"

Tim nodded. "How are you going to pay for it, though?"

"We could leave IOU's, so our parents could pay for it when they get back."

"What if they never come back? Who's going to pay for all that food then?"

Several of the kids groaned. Tim charged you interest if he loaned you money for the vending machines at school.

"For crying out loud, they'll be back, Tim." I was trying to sound positive, but I wasn't quite sure I believed what I was saying.

"What if you like it like this? What if you don't want your parents back?" George Tunnel shouted. "I can think of a lot of things I can do now that I couldn't do with them in the house, like eat all the pizza I want and stay up all night watching television."

I took a deep breath. "That'll get old after a while, George!" I shouted.

I knew that if something didn't happen soon, though, what George had suggested would begin to sound more and more appealing to a lot of the kids, and we might never see our parents again.

After a few more arguments, it was finally decided that, at least for the time being, we should all go home. The plan was to wait until the kidnappers—or whoever had our parents—telephoned us and told us what to do.

2

Pattie and I decided to stay together at her house. It had a big backyard, which was fenced in, for one thing, which meant David and Daniel would have more room to play where we wouldn't have to worry about them. I had also remembered that Mom hadn't gone to the grocery store this week, so we didn't have a lot of food at my house. I could have asked Tim Luland to open up the grocery store for me, but I didn't want to do that now. Anyway, Pattie always seemed to have some really interesting things to eat at her house.

"Do you think the kidnappers will call us and tell us where our parents are?" Pattie whispered to me, as we were walking back to her house.

I shrugged. "That's the way it happens on TV." Even though I was wondering where we'd get the money to pay a ransom, I added, "I hope they do, because I don't have any idea where to start looking for them."

If you live in a normal town, all you have to do is pick up the telephone and call the FBI, but the telephones in Broxton don't work that way. Only parents can call outside town, because you have to dial an access code before you can reach any other place, and parents are the only ones who know them.

Just as we started to cross the street to Pattie's house, two more cars raced down it and we had to jump back.

"Creeps!" I yelled at the drivers.

Of course, they didn't hear me, but I felt better.

"I wouldn't do that if I were you," Pattie whispered.

"They're going to kill somebody before this is over," I said.

"They can do whatever they want to do. There's no one to stop them," Pattie said. "Just remember that."

She was right. I probably should keep my mouth shut, but that was hard for me to do.

We went inside. Pattie's refrigerator didn't disappoint me. We ate, then put David and Daniel out in the backyard. They were soon running around, squealing with delight.

Then Pattie and I lay down across the bed in her room.

"What'll we do if the kidnappers don't call us, Mary?"

I sighed. "I'm not so sure they've really been kidnapped, Pattie."

"What do you mean?"

"Have you ever thought that this could have something to do with their jobs?"

"How?"

"Well, our parents are always working on secret projects. We all know that some of them are even working with chemicals. Maybe they just got vaporized."

"*Vaporized?*"

"Yeah, like *poof!*" I snapped my fingers to demonstrate.

"I don't believe you." She turned away. "I don't want to believe you."

"It doesn't matter whether you want to believe me or not. We have to face the facts. They're gone. Anything could have happened to them. We have to consider every possibility!"

"They're out there somewhere, Mary. I know they are. We just need to come up with a *real* plan to find them."

Finally, just as it started to get dark we decided that no kidnappers were going to call and that the next day, bright and early, we'd start looking around town for footprints or *something* which might show us where our parents had gone.

After we fed David and Daniel their supper, Pattie turned on the TV, but my eyes wouldn't focus.

17

"I'm exhausted," I said.

Pattie yawned. "You know something? I've decided this is all a very bad dream, and that we're going to wake up in the morning and it'll be all right."

"It isn't a dream, Pattie. It's real. I think the only reason we're not already crazy is that we're in a familiar house, with food and television and all the things we're used to having around us, except our parents. If anything else is taken away, though, we'll probably start losing it." I stood up and stretched. "I'm going to bed."

"Me, too," Pattie said.

Since we'd put David and Daniel in the guest bedroom and Patty had a twin bed in her room, that left only her parents' bedroom, which I didn't feel like sleeping in, because people had disappeared from it. I decided to sleep on the sofa.

Pattie got me some sheets, a blanket, and a pillow.

I lay down, but stayed wide awake. It was the first time I'd had time to *really* relax and think straight since waking up this morning. My mind was racing.

How could all the adults in one town just disappear? Why would they disappear? Did they all get together and decide they'd had enough of us kids and . . . Oh, that was stupid. I had a pretty good relationship with my parents. I'd get irritated with them at times, just like yesterday, and they'd get irritated with me, but never enough to make them dump me. At least, I didn't think so.

There had to be a rational reason for this. There just had to be!

Tears began welling up in my eyes. I hadn't wanted Pattie to see me cry, but now I didn't care. If I could only figure it out, then I'd—

I shot up. Somewhere, outside, I had heard a noise. My heart felt like it was in my throat. Moonlight was coming through the window, so it was easy to find my way through the dark room and look out. At first, I couldn't see anything, but then *it* appeared.

I screamed and backed away.

I heard feet running toward me.

"Mary!" It was Pattie. "What's wrong?"

I found my voice. "There's something out there. It looks human except that there's something wrong with its head!"

"What? You're kidding," Pattie whispered. "Someone has to be playing a joke on us!"

"No. Look!" I didn't want to look again myself, but I held the curtain open for her.

"I don't see anything," she finally said.

Then we heard a noise at the back of the house. "Did you lock all the doors?"

There was a quick intake of breath from Pattie. "No, I was so tired, I didn't even think of it."

I grabbed her hand. "We have to see what's out there."

"Maybe we should just grab the kids and run out the front door," Pattie whispered.

"No, there might be more of those things waiting for us out front. Whatever it is, we have to get rid of it somehow." I looked around. "Do any of these other doors lock?"

"I don't think so," Pattie whispered.

"Well, come on, then. We've got to do *something*!" I was frantically looking around for a weapon of some kind. "We can't just wait here until *it* comes to get us!"

We slowly made our way toward the back of the house.

We went through the living room, the kitchen, and finally reached the den, which had sliding glass doors that opened onto the backyard.

The doors were open, and moonlight was streaming into the room.

Standing there, framed in the blowing curtains, was *something* that had a strange-looking head. It seemed to be all flat on top. I was frozen to the spot, and I knew my mouth was hanging wide open.

"Who are you?" I finally managed to say.

Whatever *it* was, it just stood there, swaying unsteadily, then it grunted.

"Answer me!" I said. "Who are you? What do you

20

want?" I was still looking around for a weapon of some kind.

Suddenly, the thing stopped swaying and began walking toward us in a kind of lurching motion. It reminded me of the Frankenstein monster in the old black-and-white movie.

"Stay back!" Pattie cried.

That didn't do any good. It just kept coming toward us.

"Stay back!" Pattie cried again. Then she ran across the room and flipped on a light switch.

For a split second, I was blinded.

"Daddy!" Pattie screamed. "Oh, Daddy!"

I opened my eyes. I couldn't believe what I was seeing. It really was a man standing there, but the top of his head had collapsed! The loose scalp skin and hair were still intact, but it was all hanging down in folds over the front of his face, covering one of his eyes and most of his nose. It was horrible!

"Daddy!" Pattie said. She started to cry.

"Are you sure it's your father?" I asked. I hadn't moved from where I was standing.

"Yes. I recognize his clothes."

"What happened to him?" I said.

Pattie's dad, if this really was her dad, had stopped coming toward us and was standing in place, but still swaying back and forth.

Pattie started toward him, but he grunted loudly and she stopped. "Daddy, what'd they do to you?"

she asked with a sob. "Oh, Mary, it is him, but his head . . . I can't stand to look at it." She started to turn away, but then seemed to change her mind.

"Daddy!" Pattie cried. "Where's Mama?"

Mr. Chambers had reached the patio door. I could do nothing but stare at him. He looked so creepy.

Suddenly, he started swaying violently and grabbed for the drapes, pulling them down as he fell.

Pattie screamed again.

Mr. Chambers rolled around violently on the floor, trying to get free of the drapes, but all the while getting more and more entangled. He was grunting and growling just like an animal caught in a net trap.

That was it! Mr. Chambers wasn't acting like a human being at all, he was acting like a wild animal!

Pattie started walking toward her father, but when he saw her coming, he growled at her. He was trying desperately to free himself. I had seen something just like this in a nature show on TV.

"Pattie! Don't!" I cried. "He doesn't want you near him!" I couldn't bring myself to tell her that he was just a trapped animal now, that he wasn't acting or thinking like a human being. What could have happened to make him act like this?

Pattie came over and grabbed my hand. "I can't

just let him lie there, all tangled up," she said with a sob.

"Nothing's going to happen to him. He'll be all right. We just need to let him tire himself out. Then we'll try to untangle him and set him free." I couldn't believe that I was talking about Mr. Chambers just like he really was an animal.

We sat down and watched Mr. Chambers continue to struggle. Finally, he quit moving and lay still.

We waited for a few more minutes, then we stood up. "Maybe we can grab one end and sort of roll him out," I said. I hesitated for just a minute. "We have to be careful, though, because he's—he's acting like a wild animal!"

Pattie gave me a strange look but didn't say anything.

We walked slowly toward Mr. Chambers. I expected him to try to spring at us any minute, but he just lay there. I couldn't take my eyes off his head. The way he was lying now, the folds of skin had fallen away from his face, revealing the flat top of his head. I gasped. It was like someone had taken out his *brain*!

"I'm not sure this is a really good idea after all," I said.

"I can't leave him like this, Mary," Pattie said.

I sighed. "Okay. We'll grab this end over here and then just sort of gently roll him out."

I picked up the end of the drapes farthest from Mr. Chambers and handed part of it to Pattie, then we slowly began to unroll him.

Finally, he was free of the drapes. He still hadn't done more than just grunt, but I took Pattie's hand and said, "We need to leave him alone for a while. I think it's best."

She nodded but didn't say anything. She just kept staring at her father.

We went to the guest bedroom to check on David and Daniel. Incredibly, they were both still asleep.

"Look, I think we all need to stay in the same room and barricade the door with a dresser or something," I said. "I know that's your father, Pattie, but it's not really your father, if you know what I mean."

Pattie nodded.

"In the morning, we'll call some of the other kids to help us with him." But I was wondering now if the same thing might have happened somewhere else. Maybe my parents had come home, looking the same way. I shuddered. I didn't want to think about it. "In the morning we'll also try to find out where your father came from. Maybe he'll lead us to the other parents."

"Do you think my mother will look like that, too?" Pattie said. It was as though she hadn't heard a word I had said. Finally, she turned to look at me.

"Oh, Mary, I don't think I can stand it. It's horrible."

It was horrible. It was a nightmare. I looked over at David and Daniel sleeping peacefully and wished I could do the same. I knew I couldn't, though.

Pattie and I sat in silence until almost dawn.

Finally, she whispered, "I want to go check on him, Mary. I want to see if he's all right."

That was *exactly* what I didn't want to do, but I knew Pattie would do it without me, so I stood up. "Okay."

We pushed the dresser away from the door, and together we walked slowly toward the den. I couldn't imagine what we'd find.

When we reached the door, I slowly opened it.

Pattie and I screamed at the same time.

Instead of Mr. Chambers, something no taller than us was standing there. It had a huge head and two huge eyes, just like the thing in my nightmare.

It raised a hand and pointed a finger at me.

I felt an electric shock.

Then nothing.

3

The sun was high in the sky when I awakened, and my head hurt like it had never hurt before. "Oh, wow! What happened?" I tried to sit up, but I didn't seem to have any muscle coordination. I could see Pattie lying beside me. "Pattie!" I called to her weakly.

She groaned and slowly opened her eyes. "What happened? Where am I?"

Finally, I managed to sit up. "We're in your house. Did you see it?"

"Did I see *what*?"

"That thing with the big head and the big eyes?"

"I think I did, but all I remember is feeling like I got struck by lightning." Pattie was trying to stand up now. "What time is it? Where's Daddy? Where are David and Daniel?"

"One question at a time, okay?" I groaned. "My head won't stand for more than that."

Finally, we were both standing.

"It's probably almost noon, I don't know where your father is, and I hope David and Daniel are still asleep."

Pattie walked slowly into the den, oblivious to my answers to her questions. "He's not here, Mary. Daddy's not here."

I followed her and could see that the sliding patio doors were still open.

"That thing must have taken him," I said.

"Where?" Pattie cried. "Where could it have taken him?"

"That's what we've got to find out and fast. Whatever it was, there are probably more of them, and they did something horrible to your father's head."

"Why would they do it?" Pattie demanded. "What did he ever do to them?"

"I don't know. I just don't know," I replied.

"Mary?" I turned. David was standing behind me. "I'm hungry."

"Oh, gosh, I forgot all about you guys."

Pattie grabbed David and headed for the kitchen. Daniel was already in there, eating handfuls of cereal from the boxes he had discovered in the cabinets. The place was a mess, but I didn't care. I was just glad they weren't crying.

"Maybe we should give them some milk and juice, too," Pattie said.

"Good idea. We'd better eat with them. There's no telling when we'll get to eat again."

We fixed some scrambled eggs and bacon and made several pieces of toast, which the kids devoured, so we had to fix another batch for us.

Finally, they were full, and so were we.

David and Daniel were already feeling at home, so when they were finished, they ran to the den and turned on the television set.

"Shouldn't we tell them to wash their hands or something?" Pattie said.

"I'll do it in a minute, but I have to tell you something else first."

"What?"

"I'm not sure you're going to believe me, but you know that *thing* we saw?"

"Yeah?"

"I've seen it before."

"Where?"

"In that nightmare I woke up from when you were calling on the telephone."

Pattie just stared at me while I told her all about my nightmare.

"The thing that wanted my brain in my dream looked exactly like the thing that was standing in the door."

"What's your point, Mary?"

"I may not have been having a nightmare after all, Pattie. I may actually have woke up during the night and saw one of the creatures that kidnapped all our parents."

"Are you saying it was actually in your room?"

"It must have been."

"Why? None of the other kids in town are missing. Why would they have wanted to kidnap you?"

"I'm not saying it was going to kidnap me. I'm just saying one of them came into my room. It couldn't have known there wasn't an adult in there."

"I think they probably know everything." Pattie stood up. "What am I talking about? I never used to believe in strange little men who kidnap people."

All of a sudden, I had an idea. "I have to go to the library."

"You want to read a book? Now? Are you nuts? With all that's going on around here, how can you—"

"Hold it. It's not for pleasure. I want to look up something."

"I thought we were supposed to get together with all the other kids to look for our parents!"

"We are, Pattie, but this might help us know what it is we're looking for."

Pattie sighed. "Okay, but hurry. I don't want to be alone. What if that thing comes back? What if Daddy comes back?"

"I have a feeling that thing came back to get your father because he wasn't supposed to be here."

Pattie looked stunned.

"I didn't mean to upset you," I said hurriedly. "That's just what I think. Listen, I'll be right back."

I left the room and hurried out the front door before Pattie could change her mind.

Outside, I stood for a minute on Pattie's porch, just listening, hearing nothing—not even the sound of racing automobiles. Actually, there weren't that many automobiles in Broxton in the first place. They all had to be brought in by cargo plane to the Broxton airport, so only a few people had them. Most people rode bicycles or just walked. Like I said, it was a pretty small town.

The silence was creepy. There was no one on the streets at all.

I started walking to the library.

For a town the size of Broxton, the library was huge. It had the usual kinds of books you'd find in a small-town library—lots of novels and stuff like that—but it also had a lot of other books that people used in their research at the government center. These were in rooms behind the main building and only certain people were allowed back there.

The librarian is Mrs. Maron. She's the wife of one of the main scientists in Broxton, but she wasn't at all stuffy like he was. She liked to read mysteries, and was always telling me about the latest one she was reading. I think she talks to me because their son Toby wouldn't be caught dead with a book in his hand!

Finally, I got to the library. I hadn't seen anyone else along the way.

I ran up to the front door and pushed on it, but it was locked. I should have realized it would be. I looked around again. There still wasn't anyone in sight, so I dug up one of the bricks lining the flower bed and hurled it toward the glass door. It cracked, but didn't shatter. I picked up the brick and threw it again. This time the glass shattered and fell out, leaving a big enough hole for me to climb through without cutting myself.

It occurred to me that I probably should be worried about having damaged public property, but I didn't think anyone would complain. I was on a mission to solve the mystery of what had happened to all of our parents.

When I got to the reference room, I went straight to the computer to access the card-catalog program. I had remembered a book that came in a couple of weeks ago when Harland and I were talking about aliens. Mrs. Maron said she thought I might like it. At the time, it wasn't something I was interested in reading. Now, it could mean the difference between life and death.

I pushed the *on* switch and the screen came up. I had never thought it wouldn't, but I suddenly wondered just how much longer the electricity and the water and all the things we counted on would be available. Right now, only our parents were missing, which was enough, but I was sure these other things which we counted on could go at any minute.

I got into the subject screen and typed in ALIEN ABDUCTION. Only one title came up and that was the one that Mrs. Maron had shown me last week.

I printed out the call number, shut off the terminal, and headed for the stacks. The book was where it should be: *True Stories of Alien Abductions*. I pulled it off the shelf and turned immediately to the illustrations in the center of the book.

My heart was pounding.

"That's it!" I cried. My voice echoed in the empty building.

There were several drawings among the photographs, and each one of them looked exactly like the thing I had seen in my nightmare and that had been at Pattie's house. I shivered and suddenly felt cold.

I turned to the front of the book and started reading. Most of the first pages were an introduction, so I skipped over it and flipped to the first account of alien abduction.

A man said he had been awakened by two things with big heads and big eyes, and had been taken to a nearby spaceship where the creatures laid him on a table, and shined all kinds of lights on him. He couldn't remember how long it lasted but it seemed like a long time. He wasn't quite sure what they did, but he did remember that a lot of other creatures kept circling the table, looking at him, and making strange noises. Finally, he was returned to his bed, and that's the last thing he remembered until he awakened the next morning. Although he had several strange marks on different places of his body, he never would have said anything about it, he told the interviewer, except that a week later he saw a program on television which gave the name of a person to contact if something like that had ever happened to you.

I turned back to the illustrations and studied the drawings of the aliens. This was it. It was happening here. All the times I'd laughed about aliens from other planets or other galaxies was coming back to haunt me. They had come to Broxton and they had taken all of our parents!

I decided to take the book with me. I needed some evidence. Maybe by now some of the other kids had seen the creatures, too, and these pictures would only confirm that they existed.

I put the book under my arm and started out of the stacks. I had only gone a few feet when I saw a shadow moving in the corner of the room. I hadn't turned on any overhead lights, but now, I wished I had.

"Who is it?"

Whatever it was grunted.

I froze. It was exactly the same kind of noise Mr.

Chambers had made last night. He wouldn't have come to the library, would he?

I had to take a chance. I started toward the shadow. The growling continued.

"It's all right," I said. "I won't hurt you."

Now, the outline of the thing was getting easier to see. I gasped. It looked like another human being, but with that strange flat head. I was sure, too, that if I could have seen it better, there would have been folds of loose scalp skin hanging down over the eyes and nose. It wasn't Mr. Chambers, I knew, because whoever this was had on a dress.

"Who are you?" I called.

Another grunt.

I walked a little closer.

Then it lunged at me. I screamed. "No! Please! It's all right."

I got out of the way just in time and the thing collapsed at my feet.

Whoever it was lay on the floor, panting.

Then it turned over, and even in the dim light I could now see that it was Mrs. Maron! She looked horrible! Her eyes were darting back and forth. They were the eyes of a trapped animal, filled with terror. Her tongue hung out of her mouth at an angle. The only thing that was different from Mr. Chambers was that Mrs. Maron had yellow-looking dust on her mouth. I couldn't imagine what it was.

"Mrs. Maron?" I whispered. "What happened?"

Only a grunt came out of her mouth, though, and she continued to lie where she was, panting.

I looked around, expecting to see one of the aliens, but there didn't appear to be anyone else in the building.

How had she gotten in? I wondered. We might need to know that later on, if we were confronted with a lot of parents all at once. I knew Mr. Chambers had gotten in when one of us had left the patio door open and had forgotten about it.

I went over to where I had first seen Mrs. Maron. There was nothing unusual. I began to follow the wall toward the rear of the building. I was hoping I could find a light switch, but I couldn't feel one with my hands. It kept getting darker and darker.

Then I saw a small beam of light.

I followed it.

I finally reached a wooden door. The bottom of it had been gnawed away, enough to allow someone the size of Mrs. Maron to squeeze through.

"So that was what was on her mouth!" I said. "Sawdust!" Mrs. Maron had gnawed her way into the room! She always did have big teeth, I remembered, and almost laughed.

How could she have known to come here to the library? How could Mr. Chambers have known to come to his house? Could it be by animal instinct? Had they *smelled* their way home, just like other animals?

35

Then, behind me, I heard a growling sound. I turned and saw a shadow lunging toward me. I moved out of the way just in time.

"Mrs. Maron!" I screamed. "Don't!"

That was stupid, I knew. She probably didn't even know her name. She and Mr. Chambers had been turned into wild animals who reacted to instinct, not to anything they had ever learned. Somehow that had to be at the heart of this. I had to believe this was what those alien creatures were doing to our parents!

But how? And why?

I had to find out!

I ran blindly past Mrs. Maron—or at least what used to be Mrs. Maron.

I found my way to the front door and crawled through the broken glass door.

It took a few minutes to get used to the daylight, after the dim light of the library.

Behind me I heard growling sounds. Mrs. Maron was coming after me.

I started running.

The streets were no longer empty. In front of the library were three more brainless parents!

They were also lurching along like Frankenstein monsters, growling at each other. I didn't recognize any of them. That was difficult to do without getting up close to their faces, and I wasn't about to do that.

I hugged the library building until I got out of their sight. I was just hoping they couldn't pick up my scent, or whatever it was that animals did when they knew an enemy was nearby. Was that what we kids were now? I wondered.

Once I got past the library building, I ran from tree to tree. Even though Broxton is in the middle of what's really a desert, the government had spent a lot of money making it look like an average American town. We have plenty of big trees.

When I reached the end of the block, I looked both ways, then I raced across the street and hid behind another tree. Three more blocks and I'd be at Pattie's house.

Then something touched my shoulder.

I screamed.

"It's just me, Mary," a voice whispered.

I turned and was looking up into the face of Harland Elkins. "Don't you ever do that again! You almost gave me a heart attack!"

"I'm sorry," Harland apologized. "It's just that I was so glad to see you coming." He hesitated. Finally, he said, "I'm scared, Mary."

"So what else is new, Harland? I'm scared, too."

But Harland had such a pitiful look on his face I regretted being so harsh with him. "I'm sorry. I didn't mean to snap at you. What's happened?"

"My mother came back this morning." He turned and pointed to his house, a half block away. "She's there now."

"Does she look like she's had her brain removed?" I asked.

Harland looked surprised. "How'd you know?"

"Pattie's father came back last night. He looked like that. And I was just in the library; the same thing's happened to Mrs. Maron." I didn't tell him that she'd tried to attack me. He looked scared enough. "There are some more of the parents down the street, too."

"What's going on, Mary? What's happened to them?"

"I'm not really sure, but I have an idea. Harland,

38

did you see anyone else when your mother returned?"

"You mean, like my dad?"

"No, I mean, like, well . . . Oh, forget it. How's your mother acting?"

"She doesn't do anything but grunt, just like a wild animal."

"That fits the pattern. By the way, how'd she get in?"

"I woke up this morning and heard something scratching at the front door. I went down and opened it, and she lunged in. She knocked me down."

"Is she just loose in your house?"

"No, she's in one of the rooms. I put a dish of water and some food in there, and then locked the door."

"Has she been trying to get out?"

"No. I think she's sleeping."

I thought about telling him that Mrs. Maron had gnawed a hole in the wooden door at the library in order to get inside, but I decided against it for the time being.

"I don't know what to do, Mary."

"Why don't you come with me? Me and Pattie were going to start searching for the rest of the parents, but I need to call some of the other kids first. We'll need all the help we can get."

Harland and I started running down the street,

keeping behind the trees. At the next intersection, we had to stop while two more brainless parents lurched by, growling at each other. I thought for a minute that they had picked up our scent.

"That looks like Aaron Charlaine's father," Harland whispered to me.

"How can you tell?" I whispered back. "With their brains removed and all that loose scalp and hair hanging down over their eyes and nose, their faces are so weird looking."

"I recognized his mustache," Harland replied. "Anyway, how can they still be alive with their brains gone?"

Harland had a point. "Well, maybe just part of the brain has been removed. I don't know."

"Which part?"

"The part that makes them human, I guess."

When the two parents had passed, Harland and I raced across the street and hid behind the next tree.

"Just two more blocks," I whispered.

"Let's take a chance and run for it," Harland said. Without waiting for an answer, he started running down the sidewalk, out from behind the cover of the trees.

I didn't think it was a great idea, but I decided to follow.

Fortunately, we didn't run into any more of the brainless parents before we got to Pattie's.

40

"Where have you been?" Pattie demanded. "I thought something had happened to you." She looked at Harland. "What's he doing here?"

I had forgotten that Harland and Pattie used to like each other. "I ran into him on the way back from the library. His mother came back this morning. The same thing that happened to your father has happened to her."

"Oh, Harland, no. I always liked your mother."

"Thanks, Pattie."

I could tell they had started liking each other again, now that they shared a similar problem. At least, it would make it easier for us all to get along now. I looked around. "Where are David and Daniel?"

Pattie looked embarrassed. "Watching videos. I hate that that's all they're doing, but I don't feel like entertaining them."

"I'm sure they're not complaining," I said.

"Mary said she had a plan to find the rest of our parents," Harland said.

Pattie looked at me.

"It's gotten more complicated, though." I told her about Mrs. Maron, this time adding all the details I had left out for Harland. "There were also some other parents lurching around the street in front of the library," I added. "They looked as though they'd had their brains removed, too."

41

Pattie shivered. "I'm not quite sure I really want to find the others," she said.

"If we find them soon enough, maybe we can keep this from happening to the rest of them," Harland said.

I hated to throw water on Harland's idea, but I kept remembering how that alien zapped Pattie and me with an electric shock. "We'll have to get them away without letting the aliens know about it, if we don't want to look like lightning has struck us all."

Harland had a strange look on his face. *"Aliens? Lightning?"*

I opened the book to show him and Pattie the illustrations. "This is why I went to the library."

"Oh, my gosh!" Harland exclaimed. "You mean that *aliens* have abducted our parents?"

I nodded. "They shoot electricity out of their fingers, too."

Harland gulped. "Well, what are we going to do about it?"

"We're going to get them back, anyway," I replied.

Pattie looked less than convinced. "Even if we can get the normal parents out, Mary, when the aliens discover they've escaped, they'll just come after them again, won't they?"

"They might try, but by then, the normal parents will be able to call for help."

42

"I think it's dumb that none of us kids has the access code to call for outside help," Harland said. "I think that ought to change."

"If this nightmare ever ends," I said, "I'm sure it will. In fact, I hope a lot of things change."

"Don't forget we're supposed to call the other kids to help us," Pattie said. "We can't do this by ourselves."

"I haven't forgotten," I said. "I was planning to do that."

Pattie and I divided up the list of kids to call. I went to the kitchen telephone. Pattie and Harland went to the telephone in her room.

All ten of the kids I called were in really bad shape. I could tell they were getting more and more scared, now that what had happened was beginning to sink in.

Only two of them had parents—minus their brains, of course—who had returned. But that was actually good news, I thought, because it meant that there were probably a lot of parents who hadn't gone through the operation or whatever it was.

Only three kids—Harry Padgett, Liz Hart, and Annie Kemelman—agreed to help us search for the missing parents, though. The others didn't want to leave. They just planned to sit in their houses and wait for something to happen, I guessed.

Pattie had even less luck. No one wanted to help.

43

"It's just as well," I said, when the three of us were together again. "With that many kids, the aliens would spot us for sure."

"When are we going to go after them?" Harland asked.

"Tonight," I replied.

"What'll we do with David and Daniel?" Pattie asked.

I looked at her.

"Okay, but I'm not staying here by myself. I'll get Annie Kemelman to stay with me. She won't mind; at least I don't think she will."

When Harry, Liz, and Annie arrived, we finished making our plans. Annie seemed relieved to be staying with Pattie.

"We had to take a detour, because there are several of those monsters lurching around town," Liz said.

"Those monsters are some of our parents," Annie said. "My mother growled at me, and there's no telling what else she would have done if I hadn't got out of the house when I did."

We went into the kitchen and fixed something to eat. Then we slept until dark. I didn't want to get up, but I knew we were doing the right thing.

Harry, Liz, Harland and I assembled in the kitchen.

I had found four flashlights in Pattie's garage and handed each of them one.

44

"What do we do first?" Harland asked.

"Well, the parents are coming back from *somewhere*," I said. "I think that somewhere is out in the desert."

"The *desert*?" Harry said.

I nodded. "If they were all still in town, I think one of us would have known it by now."

"Aren't there mine fields out there?" Liz asked.

"They don't start for about ten miles," Harland said.

I wondered how in the world Harland knew that, but I didn't take time to ask. "If we see one of the parents coming in from the desert, then we can just backtrack until we find the rest of them." I looked over at Harland. "At least for ten miles, I suppose we can."

Harland nodded.

I was getting more and more curious about the location of these land mines, but I still didn't say anything.

Liz and Harry seemed agreeable to the plan.

I checked on Pattie and Annie before we left. They were both sleeping in her room. Annie had made herself a pallet on the floor next to Pattie's bed.

Then I checked on David and Daniel, who were sleeping soundly in the guest bedroom. I thought once about moving them to Pattie and Annie's

45

room, but then decided against it. I had the feeling
the aliens weren't interested in little kids.

Finally, I thought we were ready.

We didn't have to use the flashlights when we
left Pattie's house, because the street lights were
still on. Everything in the town was run by computer, and I guessed as long as it was still function-
ing, we'd have the essentials. I wondered why the
aliens hadn't just turned everything off, but maybe
that had nothing to do with why they had kidnapped our parents.

Broxton just sort of ends at the desert. It's hard
to see with all the trees and other vegetation, but
there's a big metal fence around the whole town,
with guards posted at each corner of the square. Of
course there was no one guarding us now.

On the east side of the fence, there's the only
gate. It's almost always open, as it leads to the
airport, which is beyond the fence. This is where
we headed first.

"I think they probably come in this way," I said.
"I don't think they've been climbing the fence." I
had visions of our parents being cut to pieces by
the razor-sharp wire.

"Who knows?" Harland said.

When we finally got to the gate, he turned on his
flashlight and began shining it toward the airport
hangars.

"Don't do that!" I whispered. "We don't want to advertise that we're coming."

Suddenly, in the distance, we heard a grunting noise.

"Something's out there," Liz whispered.

There was enough moonlight that we could see from the gate to the hangars. We didn't need the flashlights yet.

"On three," I whispered, "let's run toward the hangars!"

"What if they're out there and we run into them?" Liz demanded.

"I don't think that'll happen," I said, "but you should be able to avoid them by keeping your eyes open."

Harland did the honors. "One, two, three!"

We all started running toward the closest hangar. We reached it without any problems and hugged the metal wall.

The grunting noises seemed to be all around us now.

Then we saw them. They were coming from somewhere across the runway. There were four adults weaving and lurching in the moonlight. They were heading toward the gate of the fence that surrounded Broxton.

"I wonder whose parents those are?" Harry said.

None of us replied. We didn't really want to know the answer.

47

"That's the direction we need to go," I said. I pointed to the other side of the one runway of the Broxton Airport.

"On three again?" Harland whispered.

"Wait," I whispered. Crossing the runway now was one of the aliens. He almost seemed to be floating. He was easier to see than the parents, because there was a white glow around him, like one of those soft-white light bulbs.

Liz gasped. "What is that?"

"That's what's kidnapped our parents," I replied.

"You're kidding!" Harry said. "Are we in the middle of a science-fiction movie or what?"

"Something like that," I replied.

"I don't want to go where that thing came from," Harry said.

"Me, either," Liz agreed.

"Look, gang, if we're going to rescue our parents, we've got to do something now," I said. "We can't worry about what might happen. We have to worry about what's already happened."

No one said a word for several seconds, then Harland said, "Mary's right. Our parents and the other kids are counting on us."

When the alien reached the gate, the four of us raced across the open runway to the other side. When we got there, we hid in the desert grass.

"It's so different out here," Liz said.

It was then I realized that none of us had ever

been beyond this area. We'd all flown into Broxton on government planes, landed, and gone straight into town, through the gate that the alien had just passed through. Beyond this was hostile terrain, full of snakes, scorpions, spiders, and aliens who had kidnapped our parents.

I stood up. "Let's go," I said.

"How far do you think we'll we have to go?" Harland asked.

"It can't be too far. Remember that our parents have been walking into town from wherever it is."

"What if we get lost?" Liz asked.

"We'll use the lights of Broxton to guide us," I replied. "I promise we'll stop when we can no longer see the town."

"I can't see anything now," Harry said.

"Shine the flashlight on the ground, just beyond your feet. We'll walk slowly."

The four of us started toward the darkness of the desert.

We hadn't gone more than a few yards when we saw another soft white glow coming toward us.

5

"What are we going to do?" Liz whispered. "It's coming right toward us!"

"Move to the right of it," I whispered back, remembering the electric shock that knocked out me and Pattie.

We started moving at a right angle to the alien.

"Won't it know we're here?" Harry whispered.

"I don't know," I said. "I don't know anything about how they think or even if they think."

Finally, I thought we were far enough away. "This is good."

We lay flat on the ground. I tried not to think about the spiders, scorpions, and snakes that might try to crawl all over us. At the moment, the alien seemed more dangerous.

We continued to watch as it floated closer to us. When it got in line with where we were lying, it suddenly stopped.

I tensed.

"It sees us," Liz whispered.

"Don't say anything," I whispered back. "Don't even move."

The alien's head made a complete circle.

"Look at that!" Harland cried.

"Harland!" I whispered between clenched teeth. "Be quiet!"

Finally, the alien started floating again. We watched until it was in the middle of the runway, then we moved back to where we had originally been.

"We need to go straight this way," I said, pointing in the direction the alien had come from.

"How'll we know if we're going straight?" Harry asked.

"Look at that star up there," I said. "We'll follow that." I wasn't quite sure if that was going to work, but it certainly sounded good.

"I think we should just get out of here!" Liz said. "Let's go back to Broxton."

"We can't, Liz," Harland said, "but Mary and I'll lead the way, and you and Harry can follow." He shined his flashlight and started walking out into the desert.

I began following him. Liz and Harry brought up the rear.

Every so often, I'd turn to make sure we could still see the lights of Broxton. They were like dia-

51

monds sparkling on black velvet. Then I'd turn back around and continue walking.

After we'd been walking for several minutes, though, when I looked back to see the lights, they had disappeared. "Wait a minute," I cried.

Harland turned. "What's wrong?"

"Broxton's disappeared." For a split second it occurred to me that maybe the aliens had turned off the lights or made the town disappear.

"Well, I can still see it," Harland said, "but just barely."

I had forgotten that Harland was several inches taller than I was. So that was pretty tall.

"You said we wouldn't go any farther than this," Liz said.

"I know I did, Liz, but if we . . ."

Suddenly, two soft-white glowing aliens materialized almost directly in front of us, hovered for several seconds, then disappeared again.

"Where'd they go?" Harry said.

"They just vanished into thin air," Harland said.

"I'm not sure if they did or not," I said.

"Then where did they go?" Liz asked.

"Maybe they went *inside* something," I said.

"What?" Harland said. "How?"

"That's what we have to find out," I replied.

We started walking again. All of a sudden something huge loomed up in front of us.

"What's that?" Harry whispered.

52

"Do you think it's a spaceship?" Liz whispered excitedly.

"No. I think it's a hill of some kind," I replied. "When we flew in several years ago, I remember seeing a hill right before we landed. From town you can't see it or anything else outside the fence, because of the way Broxton's laid out and because of all the heavy vegetation. I'd forgotten about the hill until just now."

I was just about to shine my flashlight toward it when the two soft white glows appeared again. They seemed to come out of the side of the hill.

We dropped to the ground.

We were close enough to them now that we could make out their features. This was the first time that Harry, Harland, and Liz had seen them up close. I was sure we weren't more than just a few feet away from them.

"Oh, they look horrible," Liz said.

"It's just like being in a science-fiction movie," Harry said.

"Unfortunately, it isn't, though," I said.

Again, the aliens hovered for a few seconds, then went back inside the hill. For some reason, however, they seemed more agitated than before, like they were expecting somebody or something. It was hard to figure out. In fact, I could have been making the whole thing up in my mind, because I wasn't even sure they had the same emotions as human beings.

"There must be some kind of an entrance up there," I whispered.

"Or maybe they can just float through solid things," Harry said. "Aliens can probably do anything they want to do."

I didn't like to think so, but Harry could be right. "Let's check it out, anyway," I whispered.

We started crawling on our stomachs toward the spot where we had seen the aliens disappear. Distance is a crazy thing in the desert, I was learning. It turned out to be farther than I had thought. When we finally got to the base of the hill, we could make out a crack in it, like something had just pulled it apart.

"How'd that get there?" Liz said.

"It looks like something an earthquake could have caused," Harry replied.

"I think there's a glow coming from inside," I said. "We'll have to get closer."

"What if the aliens see us?" Liz said.

I pretended I didn't hear her and started walking in a crouch toward the entrance.

The three of them followed.

When I got there, I could see that there was either some kind of light back in the tunnel or that there were a lot of aliens standing together making the glow.

I did know one thing, though. The two aliens that had appeared twice weren't standing near the entrance or there would have been even more light.

"Come on!" I whispered. "Let's go inside."

I stood up and went through the entrance, before anyone could say anything.

Just a few feet inside, the cave widened, and it was easy to stay close to the sides and not be seen.

"This is crazy," Harland whispered behind me. "The same thing is going to happen to us that's happened to our parents. They'll take out our brains!"

"He's right, Mary," Liz said.

"I don't think so," I replied. "If they had wanted our brains they would have taken us when they kidnapped our parents."

"Well, why are they doing it just to our parents, then?" Harry said.

"Think about it, Harry. We're out here in the middle of a desert. Our parents are working on top-secret projects for the American government. They're so secret that no one knows we're even here."

"You mean they've been kidnapped because of what they *know*?"

"What else could it be?"

"We don't know anything," Liz said. "That's why they haven't taken our brains!"

Speak for yourself, Liz, I thought.

Suddenly the light in the tunnel started to get brighter.

"They're coming back out," I whispered.

We tried to melt into the side of the cave, getting as flat as we could. Since our faces were to the wall, I couldn't see anything, but it was easy to tell when they passed by us, as the light got its brightest, and then started to recede.

When I thought they had gone outside the tunnel, I said, "Now's our chance."

I started moving faster along the side of the cave, heading toward the brighter light at the back. I had no idea what we'd find, but now we were between the two aliens and whatever it was, so we had to keep moving!

"I think those two are guards or something," I whispered, as I continued to feel my way along the side of the cave.

We had only gone a short distance, when we heard a noise at the entrance to the cave. At first, it was a kind of humming sound, but that was followed by a lot of grunting noises, and then the light began to get brighter.

"Stop!" I hissed at the others.

The four of us flattened ourselves up against the side of the cave again, but this time I had my back to the wall. I wanted to see what was happening.

In the glow of the two alien guards, I could see three parents, their heads were flat where their brains should have been. I watched in horror as the aliens prodded them along like animals, using the bolts of electricity that came from their fingers.

I held my breath.

I thought I was about to pass out when they finally left my line of vision.

"That must be why the aliens keep coming into town," I said. "Our parents keep escaping, and they go after them to bring them back."

"If our parents don't have brains, then how do they know how to get back to Broxton?" Liz whispered.

"They must have part of their brains left," I said, "but just the part with instinct. They don't seem to have any human knowledge."

"In other words, Liz, our parents *smell* their way back to Broxton," Harland said.

"Exactly," I replied.

"That's terrible," Liz said.

"Why do the aliens care if they escape?" Harry asked. "They've already taken their brains out. What else can they do?"

I thought for a couple of seconds. "They probably don't want us kids seeing them until they've gotten all the information they want."

The light in the cave was getting brighter. It was easier to tell now that this wasn't really a natural cave but something that had been formed by a crack in the side of the hill. Everything was kind of jagged looking.

Finally, we reached the edge of the entrance.

"Look at that!" Harry exclaimed.

What lay beyond was similar to a big room I had seen once at Carlsbad Caverns. Because of that visit, I knew that an earthquake or something else cataclysmic had made a natural entrance into what was a huge underground cave. I could see the pointy stalactites hanging from the ceiling, and the stalagmites on the cavern floor.

Any other time I would have been awed by its beauty, but now, in the middle of this big room, was a large object that looked just like every flying saucer I had ever seen in the movies, except it wasn't as large as I had thought it would be.

I counted twenty aliens floating around the ship, busily doing different tasks.

"Where are our parents?" Liz asked.

"I don't see them anywhere," Harry whispered.

I kept looking, but I finally had to admit that they were nowhere around that I could see.

"You mean we came here for nothing?" Harland asked.

I shook my head. "They have to be here some-where. Remember those other parents came down through the tunnel. They have to have been taken somewhere."

"Maybe they're on the other side of the space-ship," Liz said.

"Maybe they're *inside* the spaceship," Harry added.

I hadn't even thought of *that* possibility. How in the world would we ever get inside that spaceship to get them? I wondered. I wasn't even sure I wanted to. What if it took off with me in it?

"I say we check the other side of the ship first," I said. "The perimeter is dark, so we ought to be able to hide behind the stalagmites without their seeing us, and find out if that's where our parents are."

I could tell this idea didn't really appeal to anyone, but it was the only thing we could do.

I made the first move and stepped inside the huge, almost circular, room. There were natural steps at the opening to the wall, so I started down them, but I tripped and went tumbling.

I hit one of the stalagmites with my shoulder and felt excruciating pain, but I bit my tongue to keep from crying out.

I was lying on my back and could see Harry, Harland, and Liz staring down at me with petrified looks. Grimacing, I gave them the okay signal, even though I wasn't sure if I really was okay.

I thought we were probably too far away from the aliens for them to have heard me, but then I realized that I was thinking about human hearing, so I lifted my head and looked toward the space-ship. I didn't see a bunch of glowing-white forms gliding toward me, so I thought I was probably safe for the moment.

Harry, Harland, and Liz were slowly making their way down the steps toward me.

"Are you all right?" Liz whispered when they got to where I was still lying on the ground.

"I think so," I managed to say, but then I realized that it hurt to talk. I just hoped I hadn't broken anything.

They helped me up.

My ankle was hurting, causing me to limp slightly, but we started circling the spaceship, keeping close to the side of the huge cavern room.

When we got to the other side of the spaceship, we saw them—our parents! They were standing motionless in a group, like soldiers at attention, but they all still had normal-looking heads!

I saw my father near the back of the formation, but my mother wasn't with him. I wanted to run over and ask him where she was, but I knew that would be a stupid thing to do.

Liz's parents were near the front. She had begun to sob quietly.

"What are we going to do?" Harland said.

I was trying to think fast.

Suddenly, one of the parents moved away from the crowd, and walking like a robot, started up one of the two ramps that led to open doors of the spaceship. It was a woman, but I didn't recognize whose mother it was.

Just as she got to the top of the ramp, a man started down the second ramp. His head was flat where his brain had been. The loose scalp skin and hair hanging over his face partially covered his eyes and nose, but we all recognized him because of that nerdy plaid jacket he always wore.

"Dad!" Harland cried under his breath.

Thank goodness he didn't say it loud enough for the alien guards to hear him!

"I have to go help him!" Harland started to run toward the ramp, but Harry pulled him back.

"There's nothing you can do for him now, Harland," I said.

"I can't let this happen to my parents," Liz sobbed.

Harry was looking frantically for his parents. "I don't see them!" he said.

We watched helplessly as two aliens met Harland's father at the bottom of the ramp and with bolts of electricity started prodding him toward the rear of the huge room.

The aliens circled the group of parents that were still standing at attention and then disappeared through what looked like an opening to another part of the cavern.

"Where are they taking him?" Harland whispered. "Maybe we can go get him."

"Look, Harland," I said. "I know how hard this is for you, but we have an even bigger problem. We've got to save the rest of the parents before the same thing happens to them."

Harland hung his head. "I know. It's just that Dad . . ."

"I understand," I said. I knew how close Harland was to his father.

"How are we going to do it?" Liz asked.

I turned to all three of them. "I've been thinking. Notice how the parents are standing in a straight line and when it's time for one of them to go up the ramp, they all move down one place and the person who was on the end starts up the ramp. They move like robots. They must be in a kind of trance and receive some sort of electric impulse that tells them when it's their turn."

"How's that going to help us save the rest of the parents?" Harry asked.

"I'm as tall as almost every mother out there," I replied. "I'm going to get in line with them."

"You're going to do *what*?" all three whispered at once.

"I'm going to circle around the spaceship and slip into the line on the other side. I've been watching, and the guards aren't paying very much attention to the parents before they go up the ramp. It's only when they come down the ramp, after their brains have been removed, that they take them away. If

I can get to the end of the line, I'll pretend to walk like a robot and then, when I get inside the ship, I'll hide and try to find out how we can put a stop to this."

Harland shook his head. "Won't they be waiting for you inside?"

I shrugged. "Maybe. Maybe not. If they are, I'll run back out and try to get away. That'll be your signal to run, too."

"I think this is a crazy plan," Liz said.

"It is," I agreed, "but it's the only plan we have."

"Why don't I do it instead?" Harland said. "I'm even taller than you are."

"Thanks for the offer, but it was my idea, so I'd better do it." I hugged Liz. "Keep watching. If you see me running out of that spaceship, then you take off for Broxton and don't look back." I decided not to tell them that the aliens could probably lay all of us out with one electric shot. I had no idea how far those bolts of electricity could travel from their fingers.

I left them and started circling around the edge of the huge room, retracing the direction we had come from. There was almost no activity on the other side of the spaceship now, so it didn't take me long to reach the other side of the room. When I got there, I was only a couple of feet away from the edge of the formation where the parents were standing at attention.

There were no aliens close by.

I could tell now that each parent was standing about three feet apart in the rows. What I planned to do was get in between the first two on this end and then work my way down gradually, getting between the next two, until I was finally at the end of the first line.

I took a deep breath and ran to the formation.

I found myself standing between Dr. Stanton and Harry's mother. They didn't move a muscle as I positioned myself between them.

I had just started to move when Dr. Stanton started edging sideways toward me. Harry's mother was moving over, too, so I did a side step for another three feet and then we all stopped.

I waited a second and then I got between Harry's mother and someone I didn't recognize.

I kept doing this until I had reached the end of the line. Now I'd be the next one onto the ramp. My heart was almost in my mouth.

I had watched the parents going up the ramp and knew I could mimic their walk.

Finally, the person on my right started edging toward me and I knew my turn had come. I began walking stiffly like a robot, heading toward the ramp. I expected all kinds of things to start happening. Out of the corner of one eye I tried to see if any of the white glowing aliens were floating toward me, ready to take me off to who knows where.

65

None were.

Now, I was on the ramp. Up ahead of me I could see through the door to the spaceship. I couldn't see any aliens anywhere, but I could see all kinds of strange-looking equipment with flashing lights.

When I got halfway up the ramp, I could hear humming noises, which I figured the equipment was making, but I still hadn't seen any aliens.

Finally, I reached the top of the ramp and the door to the spaceship. I almost turned and ran back down, but I bit my lip and kept on going.

Now I was inside the ship. I kept walking like a robot, so that any aliens looking up from the cavern floor wouldn't see me moving too fast, but when I was away from the door, I ran behind one of the two flashing-light machines.

There were still no aliens around.

I looked around quickly and saw that I was in a small room. The only things in it were the two huge box-like machines. There were three other doors, but only one of them was open. I knew I needed to plan my next move, but before I could do anything, an alien floated through the open door. It hovered for just a minute, turning its head completely around, then floated toward the door I had just entered. It let out a high-pitched noise. Down in the cavern, I heard other high-pitched noises.

The alien at the door stayed there for just a minute, then, seeming satisfied by what had happened below, floated back through the door into the next room.

I didn't realize how long I'd been holding my breath. I let it out in a long hissing sound.

Suddenly one of the parents, a father, appeared at the door to the spaceship, entered, and then started toward the door the alien had floated through.

That must be where they do it! I thought. That must be where they take out their brains!

I watched as the grown-up got closer to the door and disappeared through it.

I sneaked over and peeked around the edge. This room had a lot of flashing lights, too, but it was darker than the one I was in. In the middle of the room was something that looked like a chair in a beauty salon. Above the chair was a huge contraption that looked like one of those giant plastic hair dryers.

An alien was sitting at a panel behind the chair. I couldn't tell if it was the same alien who had floated through the room where I had been hiding, but I thought it probably was since I didn't see any others.

The man who had come through the door was just now sitting down into the chair. When he was seated, the alien pushed a button. The hair dryer buzzed and started moving down toward the man's head.

Finally, it covered it.

Oh, my gosh! I thought. This is it!

The alien pushed another button.

The parent got a strange look on his face.

What happened next was horrible. Slowly, the skin and hair on top of the parent's head began to droop, covering his eyes and part of his nose.

Finally, the machine stopped.

The alien pushed a third button and the hair dryer lifted from the parent's head.

Now this man looked just like all the other parents who had had their brains removed.

Then the parent stood up slowly, made some grunting noises, and started walking away from the chair in the opposite direction. He wasn't walking like a robot now. He was stumbling about like a wild animal that had been drugged.

He continued to grunt and growl as he disappeared through the opposite door, probably to go back down the other ramp, I guessed.

I watched as the alien removed the hair dryer, took it over to a counter, and began pouring the contents into a big jar.

Its back was turned to me.

Now's my chance! I thought. I raced across the room behind the parent who was leaving.

I could see that he had reached the door at the top of the second ramp, but he had begun to grunt a lot and was just standing there.

Below, there was a high-pitched noise.

But the parent only grunted louder and began looking around wildly.

Then a bolt of electricity zapped him.

He stood stunned and dazed for just a few seconds and then finally started walking slowly down the ramp.

I hurried to the door and peeked out.

At the bottom of the ramp, two aliens were hovering, waiting for him, obviously ready to take him to wherever they were keeping the other parents whose brains had been removed.

I had to hurry. I knew one of the parents whose brain was about to be removed was coming up the first ramp right now. I needed to be out of the spaceship before the parent's brain was removed, and also before the brainless parent started down the second ramp. It had to be timed just right.

Finally, the brainless father reached the bottom of the ramp. He was becoming agitated again.

The two aliens started prodding him with bolts of electricity from their fingers.

Now their backs were to me.

I took a deep breath, made a crazy-looking face, hunched my shoulders, so I'd look all distorted, and started walking down the ramp. I even grunted and growled a little.

When I got to the middle of the ramp, I turned my head just a little to the right, so I could see Liz, Harry, and Harland, and that's when I saw two aliens leading them away.

My heart almost stopped.

I wanted to run down the ramp after them, but I knew that wouldn't do any good.

I picked up my pace just a little, though. I needed to get off the ramp and into the darkness of the cavern edge before the two aliens returned from taking away the father whose brain had been removed.

I noticed something else that was strange. The aliens who were leading away Liz, Harry, and Harland didn't seem as tall as the other aliens I had seen. What was going on here?

Finally, I reached the bottom of the ramp. No other aliens were paying any attention to me. I guess they weren't expecting a brainless parent at this very moment. I sidestepped over to the edge of the cavern and hid behind a stalagmite for just a second.

Then I started running along the wall, hugging it closely, trying to catch up to the two aliens that had Liz, Harry, and Harland.

They disappeared through another entrance. I started running toward it. I couldn't lose them!

When I got to the entrance, I could see a narrow passageway and I could still see the aliens and Liz, Harry, and Harland.

Then they turned into another room toward the end of the passageway, and I lost sight of them.

I quickened my step.

Although it was dark, I was totally exposed now.

70

If any of the aliens came this far into the passageway, they'd see me for sure, and it would all be over.

I reached the entrance to the room, and peeked around the edge. It was full of the smaller aliens. The only light came from their glow. Liz, Harry, and Harland were standing in the center of the room.

These smaller aliens were floating around them. They looked excited about something.

They were all making high-pitched noises. I was sure now that this was the aliens' language.

"What do you want with us?" Harland demanded.

"Who are you, anyway?" Liz said.

"Why are you doing this to our parents?" Harry said.

They were answered by more high-pitched sounds.

"Can't you say something so we can understand it?" Liz cried out.

"I speak English," one of the aliens said. "I studied it for this trip."

"Why did you bring us here?" Harland asked.

"Our parents want the brains of your parents," the alien said. "We adolescent aliens want your brains!"

Oh, my gosh! I can't let this happen! I thought to myself. If everyone in Broxton becomes brainless, no one would know it for months, because it's a top secret place. The town could just disappear!

I had to get help!

71

7

I made it out of the passageway and back into the main cavern without being seen.

Now I had to get out of the hill and back to Broxton to rally the rest of the kids into action before Liz, Harry, and Harland lost their brains!

The parents were all still lined up at attention.

As I began circling the huge cavern room, I could see one parent going up the first ramp and another parent coming down the second ramp.

I knew the secret to stopping this was the hair-dryer gizmo. If Liz, Harland, and Harry hadn't been taken hostage, my plan had been to get back in line; walk up the ramp; take a seat in the chair; and then, before the hair-dryer could lower onto my head, do something to destroy it. Now, because of their capture, some more parents would have their brains removed, because, in order to pull off my new plan, I needed someone to help me distract the aliens.

I finally made it to the entrance on the other side of the huge room, but this would be the tricky part, because I'd have to dodge the two alien guards.

At the moment, no one seemed to be around.

I started up the natural staircase and then I saw a glow coming toward me.

I flattened myself against the wall and waited. The glow kept getting brighter and brighter.

Then one of the brainless parents came through the entrance.

"Mother!" I gasped.

A bolt of electricity drowned out my voice, though, as the two alien guards prodded my mother into the huge cavern room.

I didn't know what to do. I felt so helpless.

Tears began running down my cheeks. I kept thinking about the same thing happening to my father.

What I really wanted to do was take her away from them, but I knew I wouldn't be able to by myself.

I waited until they were almost to the center of the room, where the spaceship was, and then I started running down the tunnel.

I used my flashlight to light the way, because I knew now there wouldn't be any guards waiting for me. At least, I hoped there wouldn't be.

I made it to the outside entrance without anything happening. It felt good to be in the fresh air and to see the stars, but I didn't have time to enjoy any of it. I had to get back to Broxton.

I started running.

My legs kept scraping against the cactus and other desert plants and were getting really scratched up, but I couldn't worry about that now. I just hoped I was running in the right direction, and wouldn't find myself out in the middle of the Nevada desert when the sun came up.

Suddenly, I saw the lights of Broxton and began running even faster.

I was onto the runway of the airport before I realized it. The aliens' hideout really wasn't all that far from town after all. I guess it had just seemed that way when we were trying to find our parents.

I crossed the runway and ran toward the gate to the fence around the town.

Once I was inside, everything that had happened began to seem unreal. I was back in a typical-looking American town, with normal houses and normal cars parked in some of the driveways and normal trees and normal shrubs. It was easy to fool yourself in Broxton.

The only thing that wasn't normal was that all of our parents, and three of my best friends, were in an underground cavern about to have their brains removed!

I stopped running and stood under a streetlight to look at my watch. It was almost two o'clock in the morning. I was tired but not sleepy. I wondered how I'd feel, though, once I got to Pattie's house.

I started walking again.

I turned a corner and was on my street. For just a minute, I stopped in front of my house and looked at it. It was hard to remember how long this nightmare had been going on.

Had it really started just two nights ago? I had gone to bed, with everything normal, and had awakened to a ringing telephone which nobody answered?

For a couple of seconds, I thought about going to my own room and sleeping for a while. Maybe then I'd wake up from this horrible dream. I decided I couldn't do that. Too many people were counting on me.

I started running toward Pattie's house, before I was tempted to change my mind.

Finally, I reached Pattie's front door.

I opened it and hurried to her room. Pattie and Annie were still asleep.

"Pattie!" I called.

Pattie mumbled something.

"Pattie! Wake up!" I shook her sleeping form.

Pattie shot up and looked around. "Who's there?"

"It's me. Mary. You and Annie need to get up!"

Annie began to stir. "What's wrong?"

Finally they were both awake. I got them into the kitchen and told them what had happened. I told them that I hadn't seen either one of their parents, but that didn't get much of a reaction. I guess it was still so unreal that none of it had sunk in yet.

"Do you think they really will come after us?" Pattie asked.

"I definitely do," I replied. "The adult aliens are taking out the brains of our parents, and these young aliens want to do the same thing to us."

"Why?" Annie demanded. "I don't know anything important."

"That doesn't seem to matter," I said. "They must just want to think like young people on earth, I guess."

"I wouldn't know how to act without my brain," Pattie said.

"You'd act just like some of our parents are acting now," I said. "You'd do everything by instinct."

"You mean I'd have to smell my way around town?" Annie said.

"That'd be part of it," I replied.

"Oh, Mary, that's terrible," Pattie said. "What are we going to do?"

"I have another idea," I said, "but it'll take the rest of you to distract the aliens." Then I explained to them how I planned to destroy the hair dryer contraption that took out the brains.

"What if you can't do it?" Annie asked.

"Then you'd better take a good look at me," I

said, "because the next time you see me, I'll look like this." I contorted my face the same way I had when I walked down the ramp out of the spaceship.

"That's awful," Pattie said. "I don't want to look like that."

"Then let's get started," I said.

Within the next thirty minutes, we called all the kids in Broxton we could and told them to be at Pattie's as soon as possible. We told them all to bring flashlights, so we could find our way to the hill. By now, even the drag-racing high schoolers wanted to help. The only ones who weren't going to come were the ones who were taking care of the little kids. We planned to leave David and Daniel with one of them.

When we were all finally assembled in Pattie's living room, I told everyone the plan of action.

"Ready?" I called, after explaining the plan.

"Ready!" everyone shouted back.

We all headed for the front door.

I opened it and immediately jumped back as Harland fell through.

"Harland!" I cried. "What happened?"

"They're coming!" Harland gasped. "The young aliens are coming to get us!"

"How'd you get away?" I asked.

"Well, they went to ask the head alien if they could take out our brains. He agreed that they

77

could take out one from a girl and one from a boy, to see if it was worth it. They chose Harry and Liz." He turned to me. "Boy, they were really mad when they found out you had been there and they had to take Liz instead."

"Why would they be mad?" I asked.

"They know all about us," Harland replied. "They've been listening to us for years from their planet. They know how smart you are, Mary. They really wanted your brain. They're looking forward to getting it."

I shuddered. "You mean they really do know everything about us?"

"Everything!" Harland replied. He looked around. "We can't just sit here, though, we have to escape."

"Escape?" It suddenly occurred to me that Harland still hadn't explained how he had gotten away. "Where?"

"The desert," Harland replied.

"The *desert*?" I said. "Harland, we're surrounded by mine fields, even if they don't start until ten miles out, like you said earlier. Have you forgotten?"

"We really don't have to worry about that," Harland said. "I'll explain later."

"I certainly hope so," I said. "I think I'd rather take my chances with the aliens than with an exploding land mine!"

Everyone else agreed.

"Trust me. I know what I'm doing," Harland repeated. "Anyway, if we can get far enough away from Broxton, then maybe they won't get us. They mainly came here to get our parents' brains, not ours. The adult aliens didn't really like the idea, but the alien kids convinced them, so if we're hard to find, then I don't think they'll bother with us."

"We can't just leave our parents," Pattie said. "We can't just run away from them."

"We have to get help," Harland said.

We argued for several more minutes, talking about how Broxton was a no-flyover zone, so nobody would ever see us on the ground, but finally Harland convinced us that his plan was the only possible solution to our problem.

I started to tell Harland my plan about scuttling the hair dryer that took out the brains, but I decided against it. It didn't seem to matter now.

Everyone ran back to their houses to get some food and water, then we met back at Pattie's.

We called the ones who were at home with younger children and told them to do the same thing. The little kids would slow us down, I knew, but we couldn't leave them here, because the aliens would get them for sure.

Finally, almost two hours after I had gotten back to town, we were all ready to leave.

"It'll be dawn in about an hour," Harland said, "so let's hurry."

"I hope we don't meet any aliens on the way," I said.

"We won't," Harland said.

I wondered how he knew that.

We all headed out of Pattie's house in double file.

"Which way are we going?" Pattie asked.

"We'll need to pass by the hill where they are," Harland answered, "because that's the quickest route to the nearest town."

I knew that Warm Springs was the nearest town, but that it was over a hundred miles away. Even though Harland was very athletic, it seemed like an impossible task to me, but Harland didn't appear to be bothered by it.

"You're awfully smug about this, Harland," I whispered to him. "What do you have up your sleeve?"

Harland grinned. "Last year, when Mom and Dad flew to Washington, D.C., I stayed here. They didn't want me to, but I didn't want to miss school for the two weeks they'd be gone. They finally agreed to let me stay. Well, that first weekend, Harry and I slipped outside the gate and hiked the hundred miles to Warm Springs. I had found a map of the mine fields in Dad's study. It's supposed to be a big secret that they don't start for ten miles outside of Broxton and only go for ten miles after that, but even I knew about that. What I didn't know was exactly where they were, but with the map I even

80

knew that. We left as soon as it got dark Friday. Since it was a holiday weekend, we didn't have to be back in class until Tuesday morning."

"Nobody knew you were gone?" I was finding this hard to believe.

"No. We got to Warm Springs, looked around town, and then started back. It was great, Mary. You couldn't believe the freedom we felt!"

"Actually, I think I can," I said. "I get so tired of not being able to go places and see other things. Sometimes I can't stand it."

I didn't realize we had already reached the gate that led to the airport runway.

Harland pulled everyone together in a tight circle. "The dangerous part starts here," he said. "We have to stay together. There's still enough moonlight to see the person in front of you, so we won't use the flashlights until we're past the hill. Be as quiet as you can. No talking. Try to keep the little kids as quiet as possible, too."

"Okay," everyone agreed, but I could tell that they were all very scared.

We started out the gate, walking across the grassy field, toward the concrete runway. I kept looking for a soft white glow that might be coming from the direction of the hill, but I didn't see one.

We finally reached the runway and I enjoyed the easy footing, knowing what it was going to be like once we reached the open desert. If we could just

get past the hill, I thought. If we could just get. . .
I stopped walking. "Harland," I whispered. "I just
thought of something."

"What?" Harland whispered back.

"We might not all have to go to Warm Springs."

"What do you mean?"

"Well, if we could get far enough away from Broxton that the aliens wouldn't know where we were,
then we could hide, and then maybe you and I could
go on into Warm Springs ourselves and get help.
We could travel faster than if all of us tried to
make it."

"You may have something there," Harland replied. He looked at me and his eyes seemed to glow.
"I think that's one of the reasons those aliens really
wanted your brain, Mary. You're very smart."

"Thanks, Harland," I said, but I wasn't sure if it
was a compliment or not.

Now, we had reached the desert, and it was
harder going, especially for the little kids.

I looked ahead of me and tried to see any alien
shapes that might be out there. It had already
begun to get just a little pink on the eastern hori-
zon. "Are we heading straight for the hill?" I asked.

"Yes, but as soon as we reach it, we'll veer around
to our right and go behind it."

"I'd feel a little better if we'd stay away from
the entrance."

"Trust me," Harland said.

82

"Okay," I said.

We continued in the direction Harland was leading us. Finally, we reached a place where I could see the outline of the crack in the side of the hill.

"There it is, Harland," I said. "We'd better start veering off to the right now or we'll be close enough that the alien guards will see us."

Harland didn't say anything. He just kept walking.

"Harland?"

Harland didn't turn around. Something was wrong here.

Then he began to glow softly and his shape began to change. His head began to grow larger.

He turned around slowly.

I gasped.

His eyes were huge and electric bolts were shooting from his fingers.

It wasn't Harland after all. It was one of the adolescent aliens.

He'd led us right into a trap!

All of a sudden, two more aliens appeared and began floating around us.

"Where's Harland?" I cried. "What have you done with him?"

The alien who had been Harland made a high-pitched noise.

"I know you can speak English when you're in your alien form!" I shouted at it. "I heard you when I was listening at the door to that room where all you young aliens are hanging out."

"We are getting ready to take out his brain," the alien said, "just like we are going to take out yours!"

Some of the kids in the group started running blindly out into the desert, but the aliens used the electric bolts from their fingers to stop them and bring them back in line.

"You cannot get away from us," the alien who had been Harland said.

"I'm sorry," I whispered to Pattie.

"It's not your fault," she replied.

"It is, though, because Harland never did tell me how he had escaped from the aliens. I should have been more suspicious."

"What's going to happen to us?" Annie said. She was watching the three adolescent aliens as they floated wildly around us. They were obviously elated that we had been so easily drawn into their trap.

"Nothing," I replied.

"What do you mean, *nothing*?" Pattie said. "You heard what that alien we thought was Harland said. They're going to take our brains out! They're going to turn us into animals."

Now the aliens began to herd us toward the entrance of the cavern with their electric fingers.

"They can't take our brains out if the machine doesn't work," I whispered to them.

"Are you still planning to do that?" Annie asked.

"Yes!" We were inside the entrance to the cavern now. "If my plan works, maybe I can save most of the kids. We'll be inside the main cavern room in just a few minutes. You two distract the aliens, so I can slip out of line."

"How?" Pattie said.

"I don't know. You'll think of something."

"Thanks a lot," Annie muttered.

We were nearing the entrance to the big cavern room. "It's coming up. Get ready. Now!"

"Where are David and Daniel?" Pattie screamed. "What happened to them?" She started running toward the back of the line.

The aliens turned to see what she was doing. They had their fingers out ready to zap her with electricity, but before they could do it, Pattie reached David and Daniel. They were with Margie Sasnak, which Pattie had known all along. She had given them to her, when we thought we were going to leave the little kids behind. But Pattie's shouting distracted the alien guards long enough, so that I was able to slip through the entrance into the big room and begin making my way along the edge. I was headed in the same direction I had gone last time, when I had gotten in line with the other parents. But when I got to where the parents had been standing at attention, I was shocked.

There was only one parent now. One man. That meant all the other parents had already had their brains removed!

I looked around. In the distance, I could see the aliens leading all of the kids around the spaceship and across the floor of the cavern room. Obviously, they hadn't yet discovered that I was missing.

I took a deep breath and ran to where the last remaining parent with a brain was standing. I had planned to get on the other side of him, so I could go up the ramp before he did, but he started walking toward the ramp before I could do it. I'd just have to wait now, I knew. I only hoped no one noticed me. I watched as the last father disappeared into the door of the spaceship. I waited for a few seconds, holding my breath all the while, knowing that at any minute I'd be discovered, but finally I started up the ramp.

I did my best robot walk.

I was halfway up the ramp when I heard David and Daniel shout, "Mary!"

My heart almost stopped.

I began walking a little faster. I was sure that it would take the alien guards a couple of minutes to realize what the twins were talking about.

"Mary! Mary!" they cried again, but the second "Mary" was muffled, so I thought that someone had clamped hands over their mouths, but I wasn't going to take a chance and look back.

I was up the ramp and into the spaceship before an electric bolt could zap me.

I ran to the door of the room where the hair dryer was. It was horrible to watch the man's brain being removed.

Finally, it was all over. The parent stood up and began to leave the room.

I waited until the alien had emptied the hair dryer of its contents and replaced it on the machine. Then I began walking like a robot toward the chair.

I sat down in it, like all the other parents had obviously been programmed to do, and waited until the alien started to lower the hair dryer.

When it was almost touching the top of my head, I pulled out one of my metal barrettes and tossed it into the gears. The machine made a loud grinding noise and then suddenly stopped. I reached up, grabbed the hair dryer gizmo, and lifted myself up out of the chair. I bounced up and down a couple of times and it began to give way.

The alien gave a high-pitched squeal and a bolt of electricity shot past me, but it didn't hit me.

I bounced up and down a couple of more times and the arm holding the hair dryer finally broke. It went crashing onto the floor, just as four more aliens came floating into the room.

I expected to be stunned into unconsciousness by bolts of electricity, but they all just stood there looking at me.

Finally, one of them spoke. "What have you done?"

"I broke your dumb machine!" I shouted triumphantly.

"That was the only brain removal machine we brought with us!"

"Good!" I screamed at it. "Now you can't take out any more of our brains!"

"That is not true. We will do it by hand. It is so time-consuming. Too bad," the alien responded.

Chills ran through me. I hadn't solved anything. I had just made life more difficult for the aliens, and I was sure they'd remember that when it came time for them to take out *my* brain!

The aliens seemed to stare at me for several seconds. They talked in high pitched sounds to each other, then the one who could speak English said, "You are not an adult earthling. What are you doing here?"

"Your children want our brains, too."

That brought another round of high-pitched noises.

Finally, the alien said, "We need to find out what is going on here. We have been so busy taking out the brains of the adult earthlings that we have not been paying attention to what our children are doing!"

"Come on, then," I said, hoping that if I led the way, I wouldn't get prodded along by the electric bolts coming out of their fingers. It worked.

When I reached the ramp, I could no longer see the kids and the younger aliens.

"They're probably in that room at the back," I said. I continued walking down the ramp, like I was in charge. The adult aliens were letting me do what I wanted to do. So far, so good, I thought.

We found everyone in the narrow passageway

that led to the room where I had first seen the adolescent aliens. I was thrilled to see Liz, Harland, and Harry. They still looked normal.

"What's going to happen to us, Mary?" Harland shouted at me. "Are they going to take out our brains?"

"I think things are going to be all right," I said. "We're here to discuss that." I was still trying to sound as though I was in charge. It made me feel better, and I thought it might make the other kids feel better, too.

The four adult aliens floated into the room and confronted the teenage aliens.

There were high-pitched squeals back and forth.

"Wait a minute!" I shouted. "Please speak English!"

All the aliens in the room looked at me.

Finally, the adult alien in charge said, "I have asked Lumnock to explain why he brought you here. Our mission was only to remove the brains of the adult earthlings to obtain the highly secret information that was in them."

The adolescent alien turned his head completely around, causing gasps from the kids who'd never seen it happen before. "I have explained to Notwal how it could benefit our planet. We know how important the information is that is in your parents' brains, but there is nothing else there besides the facts. If we take the happiness that we have seen

90

in your brains and mix it with the information that we found in your parents' brains then we would have the perfect combination."

I didn't know what to say. I didn't have an argument for that. In fact, I had often told my parents that they were too serious, that they needed to loosen up, but they told me that that wasn't the way adults acted. Now here we had an alien kid from another planet telling me the same thing.

"Even though this is a good idea, this is not the mission we are charged with," Notwal said. "I shall have to contact our planet for further instructions."

I crossed my fingers.

"I think we should experiment first," Lumnock said. "We should take the brain of one of the children and mix it with the brain of one of the adults and see what happens." He was looking straight at me. "That way we will be able to report our findings when we contact our planet."

Notwal thought for a few minutes.

I held my breath.

Finally, Notwal said, "No, we will contact our planet first. Do not forget all of the trouble Teser got into when he disobeyed orders on Venus!" Notwal turned to me. "Come!"

The adult aliens began floating out of the room. I followed reluctantly.

When Notwal reached the door, he stopped and turned back to face Lumnock. "If you try to remove any of their brains before I get back, you will be in serious trouble!"

He'll be in serious trouble, I thought. That's a laugh.

I did my best to keep up with the adult aliens. Now that we seemed to be on pretty good terms, I decided to get as much information out of them as possible, just in case they got the go ahead from their planet to take out our brains. If we had to make a break for it, I wanted to take as many parents along as I could possibly find. "Where do you keep all of the brainless parents?" I ventured.

"We keep them in another chamber here in the cavern," Notwal said, "but we have not been totally successful in that. They keep escaping. We are absolutely amazed at the amount of instinct that is left in the brain when we've removed the information that we wanted."

"What do you mean?"

"I mean, we do not have that sort of thing on our planet. Your parents must really care about you. We do not understand that."

I didn't know what to say now, so I just followed Notwal into the big cavern room and toward the spaceship. We went up the ramp and once inside the ship headed toward a room I'd never seen before.

Notwal stood in front of a door, which opened automatically. When we were all inside a room, the door to it closed behind us automatically. We did this four times, making all kinds of twists and turns, as we went deeper and deeper into the ship. By the time we reached the last room, I was beginning to get scared. If the answer from the planet was "Yes, go ahead and take the brains out of the kids," there was no way I could escape. I was totally lost.

I wished now that some of the other kids had come with me. Maybe we could have held hands or something like that, which was really stupid, because maybe, just maybe, now that the adult aliens had left them behind, they'd have a chance to escape.

The room we were in had a huge screen on the wall and a control panel below it. In front of the panel was a big swivel chair. It was like the inside of every spaceship I had ever seen on television.

"What do we do now?" I asked.

Notwal didn't answer but instead sat down in the swivel chair and started pushing all the buttons. The panel turned into a light show, flashing all different colors of the rainbow.

Suddenly, a face appeared on the screen. It looked like all the rest of the other aliens, with a huge head and two huge eyes, but there was one difference. This alien's skin was wrinkled. It was obvious this alien was very old.

Notwal started talking to it in high-pitched tones.

It sounded like they were playing musical scales on some strange instrument.

Notwal and the old alien talked back and forth for several minutes, with Notwal getting more and more agitated. I could tell that the old alien was getting very angry.

Finally, Notwal screamed a high-pitched noise, pushed one button, and the old alien disappeared.

Notwal stood up and turned to me. "We must leave at once! Our planet is under attack!"

He floated past me, followed by the other adult aliens. Now they were all talking back and forth in high-pitched tones, ignoring me.

When they reached the top of the ramp, they floated down faster than I had ever seen them move, all the while talking in these high-pitched tones.

Suddenly, there was a flurry of activity, as aliens from all over the cavern began floating wildly around, picking up things and heading toward the spaceship.

I had just reached the bottom of the ramp when the engines of the ship started whining.

The aliens seemed to be moving faster and faster. Several times I had to duck as they floated rapidly toward me, but they maneuvered around me just in time.

Within what seemed like just a few seconds, all of the aliens were in the spaceship. The engines reached such a high-pitched scream that I had to cover my ears.

I ran toward the entrance to the passageway that led to where the rest of my friends were. When I reached it, I stopped and turned around just in time to see the spaceship lift off the ground, turn on its side, and then shoot out through the entrance to the cavern. Just enough natural light seeped in through cracks in the ceiling so I could still see several feet in front of me.

For a moment there was total silence, then suddenly all the kids ran screaming into the room, dodging stalagmites, jumping up and down, and hugging each other.

"They're gone!" they shouted. "They're gone!"

Before I could explain what had happened, though, we heard loud grunting and growling sounds at the back of the huge room.

Our missing parents had appeared.

We all stood there, looking at our parents. Every one of them had flat heads, where their brains had been removed, and the loose scalp skin hung down in folds, sometimes hiding at least one of their eyes and covering parts of their nose.

In the dim light of the cavern, they could have passed for movie monsters.

"They look terrible!" someone cried.

"They scare me to death!" someone else shouted.

"What are we going to do with them?" everyone kept asking.

I didn't have an answer to that question, but I said, "We'll take them home and then figure out what to do."

That seemed to satisfy everyone.

We made a circle around the grunting and growling parents and began herding them out of the cavern.

Things went all right until we reached the opening to the outside and then they began to get rest-less, pawing at the ground and running around in little circles. The sun was incredibly bright and seemed to be bothering their eyes.

"Keep everyone together!" I shouted.

I kept running the perimeter, like one of those cowgirls in western movies on television, who was trying to make sure none of the cattle strayed from the herd.

Once in a while, a parent would get loose and start running out into the desert, but for the most part, they all stayed together.

"Oh, Mary, it's terrible," Pattie said with a sob. "I can't look my parents in the face!"

"You'll have to," I said. "You're going to have to take care of them until we can figure out what to do."

Finally, we reached the airport runway. I was glad for the surer footing. It also seemed to help calm the parents.

Once we were inside the gate to Broxton, I stopped everybody. "What you need to do now is take your parents home, make sure they have some food and water, and then lock them in their bed-rooms. Those of you who've been taking care of small children will need to take their parents home with you, too."

"We need to hurry, Mary!" someone shouted. "My parents are getting restless."

I had noticed that the grunting and growling was getting louder. "Tonight, I'll meet with some of you about hiking to Warm Springs for help, like we talked about before."

There was a murmur of agreement, and then we all started pulling our parents out of the herd.

Some of the parents began to get quite angry, and I knew it was going to be a long and possibly dangerous night for a lot of us. But the only way we could solve this was to let each one of us take care of our own parents, and then call one of the rest of us if there was a serious problem.

Pattie and I got our parents, as well as David and Daniel's, and then started down the street together.

Even though I had already seen my mother in the dim light of the entrance to the cavern, I had put off trying to find her and my father in the herd of parents, because I didn't know how I'd react, but when I finally saw them both, I hardly recognized them.

"Mom? Dad? Are you all right?"

They grunted at me and started lurching around in circles. Dad even growled a couple of times.

"Do you think they'll bite?" Pattie asked.

"I hope not," I said. Behind me, though, Mom had started to growl, too.

By the time we got to my street, they were snarling at each other and at us.

"Maybe they're just hungry," I said.

Then we heard screams somewhere in the neighborhood.

"What's that?" Pattie said. I could tell that she was scared.

Her mother growled at her and then snapped at her hand.

"Ouch!" Pattie cried. "Mom bit me!"

I was beginning to wonder now whether my plan was going to work. "Make sure you put some medicine on that when you get home," I said, "because human bites can be dangerous." It occurred to me, however, that we really couldn't think of them as humans anymore. I felt a lump in my throat.

The screams were getting closer.

Suddenly, Carol Yackton came running down the street, with her parents chasing her, snarling and growling and baring their teeth.

My dad started to follow them, but I pulled him back by the arm. He snapped at me, but I moved my hand out of the way just in time.

"No, Dad!" I commanded.

He snarled some more, but stayed where he was.

"Shouldn't we try to help her?" Pattie cried.

Before I could reply, Harland came racing down the street. "Which way did Carol go?"

We pointed.

"I've already locked up my parents, so now I need to help her," he called as he disappeared around the corner.

"Come on, Pattie, let's get our parents home, before they decide to do the same thing."

Pattie hesitated for a few seconds. Finally, she said, "I don't think I can make it to my house by myself." She looked at David and Daniel and their parents, who had been tagging along behind us, all looking like orphans. I was sure the boys hadn't even recognized their parents and were probably wondering why all these adults with strange-looking heads kept growling and snarling.

"Stay with me, then, if you'll feel better," I said. "There's not as much food at our house as at yours, but we can take care of that later."

I didn't have to convince Pattie that it was a good idea.

We herded the three sets of parents up the steps of my house and into it. We put Pattie's parents in our guest bedroom and David and Daniel's parents in Dad's study.

I put my parents in their own bedroom.

Dad didn't want to go and snapped at my hand again. His teeth made marks but didn't cut the skin.

Finally, after we had given them all what little food I could find in the house, we locked them in.

Pattie and I sat in the living room, listening to them growl and paw at the door. It was horrible.

Finally, Pattie said, "Maybe they're still hungry. I'm going to my house to get some food."

"Good idea," I said. If food would quiet them down, then I was all for it. The growling and scratching was beginning to get on my nerves.

"Do you need some help?" I asked. Actually, I was really hungry, too, and I'd like nothing better than to pick out what I wanted to eat from the full cupboards at Pattie's house.

"No. You stay here with David and Daniel. Anyway, I just need to be by myself."

Outside we heard some more screams and looked out to see parents running wildly down the street, grunting, growling, and baring their teeth.

"I'm not quite sure this is such a good idea," I said. "You might get hurt."

"I'll be careful," Pattie said. "It'll be all right."

Reluctantly, I let her go.

I knew she just wanted to get away from listening to the animal sounds her parents were making. I wasn't quite sure how much longer I could stand it, either.

I turned on the TV for David and Daniel. They hadn't said anything since we got here. I felt sorry for the little kids. They might not ever get over what was happening to them.

Our parents had now started to bay, sounding like wolves in the north woods, so I got up and went into the kitchen, shutting the doors behind me, and picked up the telephone.

I dialed Harry's number.

101

It didn't answer.

I dialed Harland's number.

It took him a while to answer, but he finally did. "How's Carol?"

"All right. Her parents scared her to death. I helped her lock them up. I guess she'll be all right. What are we going to do now, Mary?"

"We'll have to hike out of here like we talked about," I said.

"What are you talking about?" Harland said. "When did we talk about that?"

"Don't you remember? It was . . ." I stopped. Of course, he didn't remember. That wasn't Harland. That was Lumnock disguised as Harland. I hadn't even told him about it.

I told him.

"They really wanted our brains, didn't they?"

"The teenage aliens did, that's for sure!"

Harland sighed. "I wonder why they left so fast?" Everything had happened so fast and we had been so busy with our parents, I had forgotten to tell everyone the real reason. "Their planet was being attacked by other aliens."

"Serves them right," Harland said. When I didn't say anything, he added, "Well, what did the *other* me talk about?"

"We talked about hiking into Warm Springs and getting help," I said.

"That's over a hundred miles away, Mary," Harland said.

"Well, if you and Harry can do it, then I can, too."

"How did you know that?"

I shivered. "Lumnock. He knew what you know. I guess he read your mind. He told us all about how you did it."

"Nobody was supposed to know that. We could have gotten ourselves and our parents into serious trouble."

"Nobody will know about it, Harland, except you, me, Harry, and Lumnock. I won't tell. I doubt if Lumnock will, either."

"The three of us could leave early in the morning and be in Warm Springs in a couple of days," Harland said. "I still have the map which shows where the land mines are buried."

"I'll be ready. Can you call Harry?"

"Yeah."

"Want to meet at my house on the way out, since it's the closest of the three houses to the gate?"

"Okay," Harland agreed.

"See you in the morning, then," I said and hung up.

I went back to the living room to check on David and Daniel. "Hungry?"

They nodded. They still hadn't said anything.

There was almost nothing in the kitchen now, so I got them glasses of cold water. "It won't be long.

It's cooking," I lied. I'd just have to wait until Pattie brought some food over.

I was just about to sit down when I heard screams outside.

I raced to the front door.

One of the parents had Pattie by the arm and was trying to pull her off the porch. Another parent was lunging toward the bag of food she was holding.

"Mary, help me!" Pattie cried.

I grabbed a broom Mom kept in the entrance closet and started hitting the parents with it. "Get away!" I cried. "Get away!"

The parents, a man and a woman, backed away, but continued to snarl and try to get at Pattie. Pattie made it to the door and was able to get inside.

I finally was able to back the parents down the steps of the porch with the broom, but like any other hungry animal, I knew they'd be back.

"Whose parents were those?" I asked Pattie when I finally got into the house.

"I think they're Joe Meerson's. He never did get along very well with them anyway. I think he just ignored what you said about locking them up. I think he's going to let them run wild in town and attack anyone who's on the streets."

"He can't do that!" I cried.

"He's doing it, and his parents are vicious, too!"

104

She was holding her arm where the skin had been scraped.

"We need to get something on that before it gets infected."

I took her to the bathroom and started looking around in the medicine cabinet. I found some stuff that Mom often put on my cuts.

Then the two of us took the bag of food to the kitchen and began preparing something to eat, for all of us and for our parents, too.

When it came to feeding our parents, Pattie and I had worked out a plan. She would go outside to the window of the two bedrooms and start banging on it to distract them. When they were at the window trying to get at her, I'd open the door, shove in the food, and slam the door shut again.

At first, Pattie was a little reluctant to go outside, but she preferred doing that to setting the food inside the door. Anyway, I doubted she'd have any trouble if she stayed in our yard.

Our trick worked, and I was able to put the food inside all three rooms without getting attacked.

When I closed the door of my parents' room, I suddenly remembered how Mrs. Maron had gnawed through the back door of the library, and I wondered if any of the parents would try to do the same. I was hoping Mrs. Maron had done that because it was the only way she could get into the library, because her instinct to do so had been so great. I wondered if it was the smell that drove her to it. She knew she was supposed to be there.

When we finished eating, Pattie and I gathered up the dishes and put them in the sink.

"Let's do them later," Pattie said. "I don't feel like it now."

"Okay," I yawned. "I need to go to bed. That hike to Warm Springs tomorrow will be difficult."

Pattie looked at me. "What?"

I realized I hadn't told Pattie what Harry, Harland, and I were planning to do.

She didn't like the idea of being by herself, but I didn't see any other way out of this mess.

I left her sitting with David and Daniel in the light of the television set.

I took a quick shower, brushed my teeth, and packed a few clothes in my backpack. I'd pack my toiletries and some food in the morning, I decided.

I set my alarm, got into bed, and turned off my lamp.

Then I noticed a soft white glow coming from underneath the door to my closet.

My heart began pounding.

Oh, no! I thought. It can't be!

Suddenly, the door opened, and one of the aliens began floating toward me.

I screamed!

"Get away! Don't come any closer!" At any minute, I expected to see the alien raise its hand and zap me with a bolt of electricity.

"Please do not be afraid!" the alien said, continuing to float toward me.

"What do you mean, don't be afraid?" I screamed. "I've seen what you do to earthlings!"

"I will not do that to you. I stayed behind to help!"

"What?"

Just then, Pattie burst into my room, looked at the alien, and fell to the floor in a faint.

Oh, great! I thought. "See what you've done!"

As the alien reached the edge of my bed, it suddenly stopped and hovered where it was. "I can tell you how to make your parents whole again."

I looked at him. "What do you mean?"

"I mean as they used to be."

"You'd do that for us? Why?"

The alien nodded. "That is what you want, is it not? You wish your parents back as they were?"

"What's in it for you?"

"I oppose the brain drain policy of my planet."

I thought for a minute, remembering all the things we kids had talked about, how we wished we could live normal lives in normal towns, anywhere but Broxton. "Well, I'm not quite sure we really want them back the way they were."

"That is your decision."

"How would you do it?"

"*You* would do it. You would send them to school again, just as though they were children, but you would accelerate the learning process."

"You mean all we would have to do is *teach* them?"

The alien nodded.

"But none of us kids know what they know."

"You can put any kind of information into their brains that you want. At this point, the brains of your parents are completely blank, as though they had just been born."

I was astonished. "Really?"

"Really." The alien held out his hand. "Come along. Let us get started!"

I screamed, thinking the electric bolts were about to come, but none did.

"Friends?"

I took a deep breath and slowly reached out my

hand. When they met, it was like touching a warm light bulb. "Friends. By the way, what's your name?"

"Harobed."

"My name's Mary."

"I know. Are you ready to start?"

I looked at my bedside clock. It was midnight. "I actually think we should wait until morning. Everyone's probably asleep now."

"Oh, yes. I forgot. We have no time on our planet. We do not sleep or eat or do any of those human things."

Just then, Pattie started to moan, so I helped her up and got her into my bed.

I introduced her to Harobed, and then I told her the plan. I could tell that she didn't fully trust the alien, and I wasn't quite sure that I did, either.

After Pattie had recovered sufficiently, I made Harobed step outside, so I could change my clothes, then Pattie and I took it to the living room. There we discussed how to return our parents to their original state, making a few changes along the way.

We were still talking at dawn. Pattie and I were so excited about what Harobed had told us that we couldn't have slept even if we had wanted to.

I had forgotten to call Harry and Harland, so they were by early to begin the hike to Warm Springs. When we introduced them to Harobed and told them about its plan, they were excited, too.

The four of us fixed breakfast for ourselves and for David and Daniel, then I put some food in our

109

parents' rooms. They didn't make a run for the door, so I assumed they were still asleep.

After breakfast, I called all the other kids in town. Some of them had had pretty harrowing nights, barely missing being mauled by their parents.

"Things will be back to normal very soon," I said.

I don't think any of them believed me, but I trusted Harobed. At least they all agreed to meet me in the town square. I arranged the meeting for ten o'clock.

Everyone showed up. Even though they may not have believed me, any plan was better than no plan at all.

I had put a coat and hat on Harobed to disguise him, so that he wouldn't be attacked when the kids all arrived. When I had everyone's attention, I introduced him.

There were some boos and hisses, but thank goodness no one tried to storm the park bench.

"Actually, our parents' brains were not totally removed," I began. "The aliens only took out knowledge. They left instinct."

There were murmurs in the crowd.

"Harobed told me that all we have to do is teach them new knowledge and their brains will return to normal size."

Now there were loud gasps.

I knew I had their attention.

"What will we teach them?" someone shouted

from the crowd. "My dad was a physicist. I don't know anything about physics."

"You don't have to teach them what they used to know," I said. "You can teach them what you want them to know."

"I want my dad to be a rock musician," someone shouted.

"Teach him that!" I said.

"I want my dad to play professional baseball," someone else shouted.

"Teach him how," I shouted back.

Everybody was beginning to get very excited about turning their parents into *dream* parents.

"The possibilities are endless!" I cried.

"When do we start?" someone shouted.

I turned to Harobed.

"You may start right now," the alien said.

I turned back to the crowd. "Can all of you get your parents to the school auditorium?"

"Yes!" they replied.

They all started leaving. A few people hung around to say that they were still a little afraid of their parents.

Harobed agreed to use his electrical fingers to prod them gently to the school building.

It took us a couple of hours, but finally we were all sitting in the school auditorium.

Harobed stood on the stage. "You must read out loud to your parents. CD's, tapes, videos, and TV won't work. If you want them to know all about professional baseball, you must read to them all of the books about professional baseball that you can find in the library. You must read to them all of the plays, all of the statistics, everything! If you want them to know all about rock music, then you must do the same. You must read to them every lyric of every rock song ever written. You must read to them instructions to play all kinds of musical instruments. Slowly, slowly, you will notice that their heads will begin to expand. When they reach full size, it is still all right to continue reading to them."

The parents were beginning to get a little restless, so some of us agreed to stay in the auditorium with them, while the rest of us went to the school library and to the Broxton Public Library for books.

By the middle of the afternoon, we all had stacks of books, and had begun to read to our parents.

Those of us who had baby-sat for all the little kids were even able to decide the occupations their parents would like, from things we had overheard.

I wanted Dad to be a writer, so I read to him all of the books on writing that I could find, and lots of plays and novels.

I wanted Mom to be a concert pianist, so I read to her all of the books on playing the piano that I could find.

Actually, these were things they had always

wanted to be anyway, but just never did for one reason or another.

Slowly, their heads began to expand, as their brains began to fill up with new knowledge.

None of us kept our parents the same, because we all wanted them to leave Broxton.

We read, and we read, and we read.

From time to time, I'd look over at Harobed to see if we were doing it right, and he'd nod his approval.

We also took turns bringing in food from the local grocery store. Tim Luland didn't even make us pay for it.

Finally, around midnight of the second day, our parents were back to normal, although they were still a little hazy about what had happened to them.

Dad kept talking about all the novels he wanted to write.

Mom kept composing sonatas in her head and wanting to get to the nearest piano.

One of the things we had all agreed on, before we began teaching them again, was we'd tell our parents that we had simply come to Broxton on vacation and that we'd be leaving tomorrow.

All of the parents kept asking, however, why we hadn't chosen someplace more exciting than a little town in the middle of the Nevada desert. We didn't offer any explanations. That would have to come later.

Finally, we decided that at least for the time being

we had taught our parents all that we could, so I walked slowly to the stage of the auditorium, looked out over the crowd, and said, "Tomorrow, those parents who are now pilots will fly us out of here, and we'll all begin new lives, which means, of course, helping our parents find new jobs. One of these days, we'll explain everything that has happened."

Then we all decided to have a party in the town square. It was exciting to see all of the kids talking animatedly to their parents, discussing what they were going to do when they left Broxton.

Around midnight, I said, "We should all go home now and get some sleep. Tomorrow's going to be a busy day!"

Everyone agreed.

I turned to Harobed. "How will you get back to your planet?"

Harobed looked sad. "It doesn't matter. I cannot go back yet. There are still a lot of brainless parents here on Earth who need my help."

"You're right about that," I said. We shook hands. "Well, best of luck!"

"Thanks, Mary," Harobed said. Then he floated off into the desert night.

When my parents and I finally got to our house, I made sure they were safely tucked away in their bed, then I went upstairs to my room and fell down across my own. I was too tired even to take off my clothes, and I was asleep almost instantly.

Whatever it was, it had a huge head and two huge eyes, and it was coming toward me, saying, "I want your brain! I need your brain!"

"No!" I screamed at it.

I turned and tried to run, but my feet wouldn't move.

"I want your brain!" the *thing* kept saying. "I need your brain!"

Far away, I could hear a ringing sound. Someone was at the front door. "Help me!" I cried. "Help me!"

The *thing* was getting closer. "I want your brain. I need your brain!"

Suddenly, the ground beneath my feet gave way, and I began falling into blackness.

I hit bottom with a thud.

"Ouch!"

I opened my eyes. It took me a minute to realize

that I was on the floor, tangled up in my sheets. I had fallen out of bed.

It had all been a bad dream.

Downstairs, I could still hear the ringing, but it was the telephone, not the doorbell, *and no one was answering it*!

DARE TO BE SCARED ...

If *Where Have All The Parents Gone?*
made you tremble,
imagine what would happen
if you *experienced* every
book you read.
That's what happens to
Charlie Stanton and his friends
in *Check It Out—And Die!*
the new Avon Camelot
Spinetingler coming in
September 1995.
Check this preview out ...
if you dare!

I had just passed Courtney Johnson's table on my way to get a second carton of milk when she screamed, "It's somebody's finger!" She pointed to her plate. There in the middle of the mashed potatoes was a human finger, bloody on one end where it had obviously been severed.

"Oh, that is so gross," her best friend, Jean Montgomery, cried. "It probably belongs to one of the cafeteria cooks!"

Courtney tried to push her chair away from the table, but she pushed too hard and toppled over backward.

Several fifth grade boys at the next table started laughing.

"It's not funny!" Jean shouted at them. "You should see what's in the middle of her mashed potatoes!" She stood up and began helping Courtney.

The fifth graders rushed toward Courtney's plate, but tripped over themselves and ended up on the floor before anyone could get near it.

I quickly grabbed the finger from the mashed potatoes and put it into my pocket.

"What's going on here, Stanton?" asked Mr. Scoville, our principal, looking directly at me.

"Courtney fell over, and Jean's trying to help her up," I said.

Mr. Scoville looked down at Courtney who was still lying on the floor. "Are you all right?"

"No, I am not all right." Courtney sobbed. "It was awful!"

"What was awful?" Mr. Scoville asked.

"There's a human finger in the middle of her mashed potatoes," Jean said. "It belongs to one of the cafeteria cooks!"

Mr. Scoville looked stunned. *"What?"* He turned around and looked at Courtney's plate with disgust. Then he took a fork and stirred the mashed potatoes. "I don't see anything in here."

I decided it was time to return to my own table. While Mr. Scoville continued digging around in the mashed potatoes, I walked away. I knew I had to slip the rubber finger to someone else before Mr. Scoville got suspicious and decided to search me.

I finally reached my table, two over from Courtney's, and showed the finger to Dustin Montgomery. "Hide this in your pocket."

"Where'd you get *that*?" Dustin demanded.

"It's a long story."

"It still has mashed potatoes on it, Charlie! Wipe it off!"

I took my napkin, wiped off the finger under the

table so no one would see me and tell Mr. Scoville, then I handed it to Dustin, who quickly put it inside his pocket.

"Charlie Stanton!"

I was sure I jumped two feet out of my seat. Mr. Scoville was standing right behind me.

"Yes, sir?"

"Stand up and empty your pockets!"

I stood up. "I think this is really illegal, Mr. Scoville."

Mr. Scoville began turning red. "Just do what I said!"

I emptied my pockets and two pieces of candy fell out. I gave Mr. Scoville a puzzled expression. "Want some?"

"I know you're behind this, Stanton. Right before Halloween you always start putting rubber body parts in people's food. You're sick, you know that? Sick! Sick! Sick!" Then Mr. Scoville turned around and stormed out of the cafeteria.

Several of the kids around us started snickering.

"That was really close," Dustin said. "Want your finger back now?"

"No, you'd better keep it for a while. Mr. Scoville may decide to search me again. Anyway, it's not my finger."

"What do you mean it's not your finger?"

"I think it belongs to that new girl, Davina Dishman. I saw her drop something onto Courtney's plate when she wasn't looking."

Dustin and I looked around the cafeteria until we spotted Davina. She was sitting in a corner by herself.

"You mean there's someone else in this school besides you who likes to play practical jokes with body parts, and it's a *girl*?"

"Yeah. Isn't it great? I wonder if she likes to read horror books, too?"

"A lot of us like to read horror books, Charlie, but you're the only one who acts them out!"

"Until now, you mean."

Dustin looked at his watch. "It's almost time for class. Come on."

I followed Dustin to the rear of the cafeteria to put our trays on the conveyor belt.

Dustin sighed. "I wish we could read horror books during library period."

"Yeah, but Mrs. Hart would never let us do that," I said, remembering the times I'd tried and all the times I'd been caught and sent to the principal's office. "Mr. Scoville still has two of my favorite books, *The Body in my Backpack* and *Body Parts for Lunch*. I need to get them back."

"Yeah, I liked those, too. Hey, that's where Davina got the idea for putting a finger in Courtney's mashed potatoes, isn't it?"

I nodded. "Except in *Body Parts for Lunch*, it was a *real* finger."

"I remember. It was great! Oh, hey, I want to

stop by the library so I'll have something to read during last hour."

We headed down the hall, entered the library, and stopped immediately.

Sitting behind the desk was a woman we'd never seen before.

"A *substitute*?" Dustin whispered.

"I hope so. Maybe she won't care what we read. I've been wanting to finish *Who's Buried in the Basement?*"

We took a seat at one of the tables in the first row. It was the only table that had two empty chairs together. Dustin and I usually sat in the back so we could try to read our horror books without getting caught.

The woman was writing something in a notebook. Finally, she looked out over the room and said, "I'm Ms. Gunkel. I'll be the librarian for the next few days while Mrs. Hart has some hospital tests done."

Dustin looked at me and grinned.

"Look!" I whispered to him. I pointed to a canvas bag on the table. I was sure I could see some Stephen King novels sticking out of it. My heart skipped a beat. *Did Ms. Gunkel actually read horror books?* I wondered. That would be almost too much to hope for. It was one thing to tolerate them. It was something entirely different if she actually read them.

I raised my hand.

"Yes?"

"My name's Charlie Stanton, and well, I was just wondering, do you like to read horror books?"

"I read them all the time. They're my favorites!"

"Do you mind if we read them during library time?"

"Oh, no. Actually, I *encourage* it."

Dustin and I looked at each other and grinned again. I couldn't believe what I was hearing.

"Do you like horror books, Charlie?" Ms. Gunkel asked.

"I read them all the time, too," I announced proudly.

"So do I!" Dustin chimed in.

"So do I!" said a voice at the back of the room.

Dustin and I turned. Davina Dishman was sitting at a table in the rear. She had a big grin on her face.

"In fact," Ms. Gunkel continued, "I plan to start a Horror Reading Club."

My heart was beating big time. After all the trouble I'd gotten into reading horror books in the past, I was now on the verge of being able to do it without any grief from any adults.

"I invite any of you who are interested in joining this club to stay just a minute after school, and I'll tell you all about the plans I have for you!"

"I'll stay!" I cried.

Right after I said it, though, I had the strangest feeling I might live to regret it.